P9-CDM-396

Our TV gets the Dead Channel

Zach clicked the channel button. "What did you do to the TV?"

The screen was all staticky, the way it looks when you put in a blank videotape. He clicked the VCR button on, then off again.

Still a lot of static, but now there was definitely something in the middle. "I'd swear it looks like a person," he said. "But why the same thing on all channels?"

"Zach, turn it off," I said.

Over his shoulder I could see the person on the TV coming in clearer every second, walking toward us through the field of static, a dark silhouette in a long gown and bonnet.

Jackie took the remote control out of Zach's hand and turned off the power.

Zach opened his mouth to protest but didn't say a word. The screen stayed the same: black and white static with someone coming straight toward us.

Closer.

Closer.

Till her face filled the screen. . . .

———◦———

"The African-American ghosts provide an intriguing counterpoint to a thoroughly modern houseful of children, who learn a history lesson strong enough to chill their bones."
—Publishers Weekly

OTHER PUFFIN BOOKS YOU MAY ENJOY

There's a DEAD PERSON Following My Sister Around

VIVIAN VANDE VELDE

PUFFIN BOOKS

PUFFIN BOOKS
Published by the Penguin Group
Penguin Putnam Books for Young Readers,
345 Hudson Street, New York, New York 10014, U.S.A.
Penguin Books Ltd, 27 Wrights Lane, London W8 5TZ, England
Penguin Books Australia Ltd, Ringwood, Victoria, Australia
Penguin Books Canada Ltd, 10 Alcorn Avenue, Toronto, Ontario, Canada M4V 3B2
Penguin Books (N.Z.) Ltd, 182-190 Wairau Road, Auckland 10, New Zealand

Penguin Books Ltd, Registered Offices: Harmondsworth, Middlesex, England

First published in the United States of America by Harcourt Brace & Company, 1999
Published by Puffin Books,
a division of Penguin Putnam Books for Young Readers, 2001

7 9 10 8 6

Copyright © Vivian Vande Velde, 1999
All rights reserved

LIBRARY OF CONGRESS CATALOGING-IN-PUBLICATION DATA
Vande Velde, Vivian
There's a dead person following my sister around / Vivian Vande Velde.
p. cm.
Summary: Eleven-year-old Ted becomes concerned and intrigued when his
five-year-old sister Vicki begins receiving visits from two female ghosts.
ISBN 0-14-131281-5 (pbk.)
[1. Ghosts—Fiction. 2. Slavery—Fiction. 3. Underground railroad—Fiction.
4. Brothers and sisters—Fiction. 5. New York (State)—Fiction.] I. Title.
PZ7.V2773 Th 2001 [Fic]—dc21 2001016052

Printed in the United States of America

Except in the United States of America, this book is sold subject to the condition that
it shall not, by way of trade or otherwise, be lent, re-sold, hired out, or otherwise
circulated without the publisher's prior consent in any form of binding or cover
other than that in which it is published and without a similar condition
including this condition being imposed on the subsequent purchaser.

To Michael—
a wonderful editor,
and a loyal friend

CONTENTS

There's a
DEAD
PERSON
Following My
Sister Around

CHAPTER 1

We *Don't* Move into a New House

MOST GHOST STORIES start with a new house. Well, actually, it's usually an old house, a little bit run-down but with more rooms than your average Howard Johnson—most of them with dark corners and cobwebs. But it's new to the people about to get haunted: The family moves out to the country or to an island dominated by an abandoned lighthouse; or the kids are sent to visit Great-Aunt Agatha, who lives by the windswept moors and talks to herself; or the car gets a flat tire or the horse breaks its leg, and the travelers are miles from anything except the gloomy mansion on top of the hill. The house is generally situated someplace that has frequent thunderstorms, preferably between a swamp and a cemetery.

Our house *is* old, but we've been living here peacefully forever. At least, my family has been here forever. The house was built by my grandfather's uncle's father—I think I've got that right. Anyway, I know it was built by the ancestor I was named after—Theodore Beatson (except everyone calls me Ted)—and he built it before the Civil War. I've been living here just about twelve years, because that's how old I am, just about twelve. Not that the house looks 150 years old. Granddad says he signed the house over to my dad and moved to the condominium in Florida because Grandma had run out of walls to knock down and floors to refinish. So it's not like the house looks spooky or anything.

And we're not out in the middle of nowhere, either. We're in Rochester, New York, which is pretty big even if nobody outside of New York State has ever heard of it. We're close enough to hear Mr. and Mrs. Lidestri arguing in the house on one side of us, and to smell the chlorine from the Wienckis' pool on the other side. Behind our house is a big ditch that was part of the old Erie Canal before the canal was rerouted about a mile south. But the ditch isn't as interesting as it sounds: There's a housing development right on the other side, close enough that in winter, without leaves on the trees, we can see their lights. We can also hear their dogs barking—summer and winter—but then again, they can probably hear my brother Zach's stereo, which only tunes in heavy-metal stations at about a thousand decibels, proving, I guess, there is justice in the world.

So, no swamps, cemeteries, or windswept moors. (Just to be sure, I asked Zach what a moor is and he said it's a black person. I told him that sounded stupid, but his tenth-grade class is reading *Othello* and he showed me where it says "Othello the Moor"; and there's Othello on the cover, definitely black. I'm not sure what's so spooky about a windswept black person, but anyway, the closest black people are the Baileys, five houses down.)

Not counting Zach, there's nothing weird about my family: no undertakers or mad scientists or people who only come out at night. My dad works for the telephone company and Mom is a waitress at the little coffee shop in the mall. Besides me and Zach, there's our little sister, Vicki, who's in kindergarten.

So that's me, my family, and our house.

No long-lost relatives have come to visit.

Nobody died.

Halloween was five months past.

But suddenly we had a ghost.

CHAPTER 2

A Ghost Moves In

THE HAUNTING STARTED so slow and easy we didn't know enough to be afraid.

Mom, who usually works only during school hours, was working in the evenings because one of the other waitresses had just quit.

Dad also would normally have been home in the evenings because he's a manager at the phone company—an indoor nine-to-five job. But the repair people had gone on strike the week before, so the management people were trying to cover for them, even though they didn't know what they were doing. All of a sudden Dad was working from seven in the morning to seven at night—sometimes later if he got in the middle of something—and when he *was* home, generally he'd be asleep or at the kitchen table, trying to make sense of the technical manuals. I can't remember which it was that particular night.

Vicki was supposedly asleep upstairs, and Zach and I were trying to watch TV together.

Except that Zach had the remote control.

It's impossible to watch TV when Zach has the remote control. Every time there's a commercial, he starts to wonder what he's missing on the other channels. Nine times out of ten it's more commercials, but that doesn't stop him. He'll hold his finger down on the button that advances the channels. Flip-flip-flip. Just about a second slower than it takes for the image to register on the eye. Very annoying. A black-and-white movie. *Gilligan's Island* in Spanish. Painting lessons. An opera about a woman who is dying, who'll still be dying fifteen minutes from now, the next time Zach flips through. By the time we get back to whatever we were watching, our commercial's ended and the show has gone on without us: I've missed the crucial revelation somewhere between Madonna on MTV and Senate hearings on C-SPAN.

When Dad is in the room, he takes the remote control away from Zach; but Zach's sixteen, and if I try to use force with him, he sits on me.

So I have a tendency not to get too involved with TV when it's just the two of us.

That's why I noticed Vicki in the upstairs hall. She was sitting on the floor, wearing a robe and her ratty gray bunny slippers, watching the TV through the slats of the stair rail.

I called up to her, "You better—"

"Jeez"—Zach smacked me on the side of the head with the remote control—"not in my ear, you jerk."

"You bigger jerk," I said, but I moved before I said it. My head must have made contact with the mute button—it felt like all the buttons were imbedded in my scalp—but anyway, Zach ignored me while he tried to figure out what had happened to the sound. I told Vicki, "If Mom comes home and catches you out of bed, I don't want to be around to see what happens."

"Keep it down," Zach grumbled.

Vicki said, "Marella wanted to see what TV's like. She's never seen TV before."

"Who's Marella?" I asked.

Vicki pointed to the empty spot next to her. "My new friend."

Well, I thought, kids pick up the strangest things when they go to kindergarten. I'm told Zach acquired a pet giraffe in kindergarten, though I only got chicken pox. Anyway, I figured one of the other kids had an imaginary friend and Vicki had decided she should have one, too.

"Well, you tell Marella—" I started.

Zach threw one of the decorative pillows at me. "You tell Marella to go to bed," Zach finished for me.

Vicki got to her feet. Disdainfully she said, "Marella didn't like TV, anyway," and she stomped off back to her room.

I should have been suspicious. From a girl who

names her stuffed animals things like Pink Bear and Big Rabbit—I should have been suspicious.

But that was how it started.

THE NEXT MORNING at breakfast, just as Zach was about to sit down, Vicki screamed.

Zach nearly swallowed the pen he was carrying in his mouth, and Mom poured out about two cups of milk, none of which landed in her coffee mug. I'd been looking at Vicki, however, and I figured I knew what it was all about.

"What?" Mom asked in her frantic mother's voice. "What's wrong?"

"Zach almost sat on Marella," Vicki said.

"Who?" Mom asked.

"Her new friend," I explained. I wiggled my eyebrows at Mom to indicate the nature of that friendship. When Mom continued to look at me as though I were speaking Martian, I added, "Her new—*invisible*—friend."

Zach, who'd frozen midsit, said, "Obviously someone dropped both of you on your heads when you were babies," and he let himself fall the rest of the way into his seat, so hard the chair skittered backward on the floor. "How's that feel, Marella?" he demanded.

In that self-satisfied tone all girls master by the age of two, Vicki said, "She already moved to Daddy's chair."

Zach, whose brain is not up to competition with

a five-year-old, mimicked, "'She already moved to Daddy's chair.'" He started poking at the air above the empty seat.

"Stop it!" Vicki screamed. "Stop it! She doesn't like that."

"If she doesn't like it," Zach said, "she should tell me to stop."

"She can't talk," Vicki said. "Stop it now!"

"If she can't talk, then how do you know her name's Marella?" Zach asked with uncharacteristic clarity of thought.

Vicki was trying to grab hold of his jabbing finger, but she wasn't fast enough. "She *can* talk if she *has* to, but it's hard. *Mommy!* Make him stop."

"Vicki!" Mom said, having finally caught her breath again. "Stop that awful squealing. Zach, leave your sister alone. Ted, elbows off the table."

That's Mom. She never wants to show favoritism, so she figures if she yells at one of us, she'd better yell at all of us.

As Mom turned her back to get the sponge from the sink, Zach gave the air a final poke. "Does Marella like this?" he whispered.

"She moved again," Vicki said. But this time she didn't say where.

"Knock it off, all of you," Mom warned, sponging up the spilled milk. "And hurry up, your buses are going to be here any second." She indicated the pen and paper

Zach had brought to the table. "Is that something I have to sign?"

"Nah, it's just science."

"And it's due when?"

Zach glanced at his wristwatch. "Twenty minutes. But there's only one essay question left. More than enough time."

I pushed my chair back, to get out of there so I wouldn't have to hear Mom's lecture.

At the same instant, Vicki lunged across the table, hitting Zach's glass of orange juice at just the right angle so that it fell over and drenched his science paper.

With a cry somewhere between pain and anger, Zach picked up the sheet and tried to shake off the juice, which was already making the orange-stained paper curl. "Why you little—"

"Zach," Mom warned, sponging the area around him.

"I didn't mean it." Vicki had gone white and her bottom lip was beginning to tremble.

"What do you mean, you didn't mean it?" Zach said. "You just reached right over—"

"I was trying to stop Marella," Vicki said. "She was going to knock over your juice for being mean to her, and I was trying to stop her."

"Dropped on your head!" Zach shouted at her.

Vicki began to sob.

One thing I have to admit: Even then, *I* thought she was convincing.

"Zach!" That was Mom's final-warning voice. "You shouldn't have been doing your homework at the breakfast table in the first place. And you, young lady, if you're going to bring your friends—invisible or not—to breakfast, you better tell them to behave themselves. Ted, don't slouch."

Outside, a bus began to beep.

All three of us scrambled to our feet, because Zach's bus comes about twenty seconds after ours.

I grabbed hold of Vicki's sleeve to get her to hurry up—it's embarrassing to have the whole bus wait for the kid everybody knows is your sister.

"I didn't do it on purpose," she repeated to Zach.

Zach, holding his homework at arm's length so it wouldn't drip on him, tapped her none too gently on top of the head to show just where he figured she'd been dropped.

She began to howl again, but fortunately she kept on walking.

None of us bothered to answer as Mom's voice followed us outside. "And have any of you brushed your teeth?"

I Learn Everything There Is to Know about Luxembourg

FOR THE NEXT COUPLE days, I pretty much forgot about Marella. For one thing, she behaved herself the rest of that first day, which was a good thing, since Dad was able to take off enough time from accidentally sabotaging people's phones to drop in for dinner, so there wasn't an extra chair. And apparently she wasn't much for eating, so—after a while and because our table conversation was boring, according to Vicki—she stopped coming at mealtimes.

Still, Vicki seemed to be spending a lot of time in her room, playing quietly, having earnest little conversations with herself. Mom and Dad thought it was cute, Zach asked if there were any other demented people in the family, and I spent more time worrying about the Social Studies Fair than about people who weren't there.

My project was Luxembourg—which just goes to show that our countries were assigned to us, since who in their right mind would choose Luxembourg? The whole country isn't that much bigger than Rochester. The year before, when we'd done states, I'd gotten Ohio. I'd written a real nice letter to the board of tourism, explaining about the fair and telling them I'd appreciate any flyers or travel brochures or other information they might have. The entire fifth grade wrote these letters to various states, and most of them got all sorts of wonderful stuff in return: postcards, state flags, bumper stickers. Ohio was one of two states that did not respond. Anyway, this year I'd written a letter to Luxembourg. Now, with only the weekend left till the fair, it looked like I was going to be stood up again.

So Friday, after dinner, I bicycled to the library to look up information about Luxembourg, the one country in the world in which nothing interesting has ever happened.

I'd already done the written report—it had been due the Monday before the fair—but I was looking for maps and interesting pictures to trace for my display. Still, all the while I was thinking about how Joe Antonio had constructed a Lego model of the Eiffel Tower, and Andrea Dittman—who was doing Scotland—had this inflatable Loch Ness Monster her dad had brought back from a business trip, and Lenny Stetzel had been telling us for weeks about the delicious Greek baklava his mother was going to bake.

The librarian suggested *National Geographic* and—hooray!—there was an article in the July 1970 issue.

(*National Geographic* has been around forever, so it's probably even done a piece on Ohio.)

Luxembourg *is* kind of pretty, but there was no way I could trace those pictures. I started feeding quarters into the photocopier.

The librarian came up behind me. I was sure she was about to tell me I was damaging the binding on the magazine and that I'd have to stop making my little black-and-white, nearly illegible copies, but she said, "Are you aware, young man, that there are several large boxes of *National Geographic* in the used-books room? The magazines are only twenty-five cents each."

For once I was lucky. Somebody must have been cleaning out their attic, because there were these boxes full of magazines—boxes labeled and in chronological order—from 1963 to 1981.

I found the July 1970 issue, paid my quarter, and bicycled home.

Now what? The judges would not be impressed by my report and a single issue of *National Geographic* lying side by side, no matter how old that issue was. I decided it would look like more if I spread it out: cut out the pictures, paste them on something, maybe draw a picture of the Luxembourg flag in the middle (three horizontal stripes: red, white, and blue—real creative), or maybe I could draw a giant map of Luxembourg and put the pictures around the inside of that.

I decided I did not want to use poster board. For one thing, we didn't have any, and if I asked my mother to buy some now, she'd ask why I'd waited so long to start. For another, I remembered that last year those of us who'd used poster board had spent half the evening picking up our displays every time they tipped over. I needed something more substantial.

After generations of Beatsons living in the same house, our basement is full of just about everything anybody could need. In fact, our basement—come to think of it—is the only part of the house that is the least bit spooky, with its packed-dirt floor and separate little cubbyhole rooms for storage. But Mom has about a dozen braided area rugs all over the laundry and work-bench areas, and it's well lighted. I found a section— about three feet by five feet—of wall paneling left over from the latest redoing of the downstairs bathroom. Just what I needed. Properly braced, *that* wouldn't sag under its own weight and fall.

I positioned the best illustrations and left space for the flag, then went to fetch a hammer and nails. The nails I found right away. But the only hammer was the rubber mallet for putting hubcaps back on after chang-ing the car's tires.

"Zach," I called up the basement stairs. "Zach!" I could hear him—talking on the phone; how come he couldn't hear me?

I trudged upstairs. "Zach, where's the hammer?"

Zach put his hand over the receiver. "Can't you see I'm on the phone?" he snarled.

Yeah, and by the way he'd been talking, I could see he was on the phone with a girl.

"I need the hammer," I said.

"It's in the basement."

"No, it's not."

Zach shrugged, his contribution to scholastic endeavor exhausted, and went back to his phone conversation.

I returned to the basement and tried pounding a nail with the rubber mallet. I missed, hit the wood, bounced off the wood, and came close to knocking myself out. The next time I aimed more carefully, but even hitting the nail didn't get me anywhere.

Back upstairs, Zach was off the phone and drinking milk from the carton, which he knows drives Mom crazy. "Have you thought where the hammer could be?" I asked him.

Apparently he hadn't heard me coming up behind him, and he choked, spitting and dribbling milk all over. "Do you mind?" he sputtered.

Zach isn't the handy kind around the house, so it really didn't seem likely that he'd used the hammer and could be harassed into remembering where it was.

So I called Mom at work, which I guess wasn't a good idea. They had to call her to the phone, and when she came on, she said, "What's happened? What's wrong?"

"Nothing," I said. "I'm looking for the hammer."

There was a long icy silence. "And you thought I might have brought it with me to the restaurant?"

I squirmed. "I was hoping you might know where it is."

"In the basement, as far as I know." She got suspicious again. "Ted, is there something wrong at the house?"

What was she picturing? "No," I assured her. "I just need it for a school project. It's not in the basement. Do you think Dad took it to work?"

"No, they gave him his own toolbox. Check the basement again."

"Right." She was just trying to get rid of me. We both knew I wouldn't have called without carefully checking the basement to begin with. "Thanks, anyway."

"Toodles," she said. "I'll be home in another hour and a half."

I hung up. All this wonderful enthusiasm for Luxembourg, and no way to use it. I knew if I waited too long, it'd go away. So I figured, *Oh, all right. Why not?*

I went upstairs and peeked into Vicki's room—Zach is the only one who closes his door: closes, locks, and barricades—with soiled laundry and week-old lunch bags. "Vicki," I whisper-called into the darkness. "You still awake?"

"Yes, Teddy," she answered. She's the only person in the world I allow to call me Teddy.

"You wouldn't happen to know where the hammer is, would you?"

"I've got it."

I saw her reach under her pillow and pull it out. I went into the room. "What in the world are you doing with that?" I had thought maybe she'd used it to crack nuts or kill spiders, but under her pillow was weird.

Weirder yet was that she wouldn't put the hammer into my outstretched hand. "It's protection," she said.

"Against what?" I sat on the edge of her bed, wondering if she'd heard something scary on the news.

"Against the bad lady," Vicki said.

"What bad lady?"

"The one who comes here at night."

"Here?" I asked, still trying to relate this to something on the news. "This neighborhood?"

"This room," Vicki said.

"Vicki," I told her, laying my hand on hers, "there's no bad lady. How could she get in here? March is too cold out for leaving the windows open—"

"She comes through the walls," Vicki said.

"Oh," I said. Then I had a sudden inspiration. "Like Marella?"

"Marella's afraid of her."

"What, exactly, does this bad lady do?" I asked.

Vicki gave me that look reserved for the very bright to give to the very slow. "She comes through the walls," she said.

Well, yeah, I guess that would have been enough for me, too. She wasn't going to hand over that hammer, I could tell. I tried a different approach. "Have you talked to Mommy or Daddy about this?"

"I told Zach. I asked if I could sleep in his room so the bad lady couldn't find me, and he told me I had to sleep here but I could use the hammer to protect myself."

Good old Zach.

"Well, could you loan me the hammer for five m—"

"Tomorrow," Vicki said. "During the day."

"Right," I said. There was no use arguing, I could tell. "Well, good night, Vicki." I felt sorry that she was so obviously worried, so I added, "And remember: Mommy and Daddy and I—and even Zach—we'd never let anything hurt you."

Vicki snorted as she replaced the hammer under her pillow. Even at five years old she knew enough to recognize that as the empty promise it was.

CHAPTER 4

Would All the Dead People Please Leave the Room?

I WAS HAVING a bad dream.

You know how in dreams you can know things that there's no way of knowing? I knew I was in Luxembourg. (See what being too conscientious about homework can lead to?) I was in an abandoned castle. The rooms were empty and huge: seven or eight times taller than me, with acres of polished-stone floor to cross before coming to a pair of golden doors opened to reveal an identical room beyond, leading to another pair of golden doors opening into another room...on and on as far as the eye could see. There was something I needed to get—I didn't know what, but I was desperate for it—and I walked faster and faster, searching frantically, my footsteps echoing hollowly. I knew—the way you know in dreams—that it was no use calling out: My voice wouldn't work.

And I also knew, though the castle didn't look particularly scary, that something bad was about to happen.

I mean, Something Really Bad.

But then I found what I was looking for. It was a hammer, lying on the floor in the middle of a room just like all the other rooms. I thought now that I'd found it, I'd wake up. But I picked it up and nothing happened, so I turned to retrace my steps.

Except that the rooms looked different, coming from this direction. They were still huge, but instead of being empty, they were full of once-rich-but-now-moldy couches and chairs. And lounging on the furniture, in equally once-rich-but-now-moldy clothes, were decaying corpses.

Well, I said to my dream self, *who needs this? There must be a back door.*

I turned back to keep on going past where I had picked up the hammer, but now I saw that there were no more rooms beyond this one. No windows, either, now that I thought about it. I had to go out the way I had come in.

The rooms I had to pass through stretched in a straight line before me, each room smaller and smaller, visible through the open doorways. Far off I could see a hint of green grass and blue sky—the safety of outside. I held the hammer close to my chest and started walking. The corpses stayed where they were. This wasn't so bad, after all.

Except that when I passed through the first doorway,

the huge golden doors slammed shut behind me, cutting off any possible retreat.

So I started running, just in case the other doors started closing, and that got the attention of the corpses in the second room. They jumped up, all bony and disgusting, some of them leaving behind clumps of loose hair and tattered finery on the furniture. They started to close in on me, their movements stiff and jerky—like badly controlled marionettes—but fast.

Zach says that if you die in a dream, it's such a shock to your system that you actually will die. I've always thought that was pretty dumb, and I'd always meant to look it up somewhere but had never gotten around to it. At this point it suddenly didn't seem so dumb anymore.

I burst through the second set of doors, and they slammed shut behind me.

The corpses in that room got to their feet.

Room after room, I fled. My heart felt as though it would burst, but in each room the corpses were a little bit faster. I could smell them—like the rotten seaweed that sometimes accumulates on Lake Ontario—and I could feel their bony fingers snatching at my clothes, each time a little bit more solid as they came closer and closer.

And then suddenly I was in the next to the last room. I could see outside clearly. Luxembourg's one mountain range, the Ardennes, towered in the distance, dwarfing the telephone pole practically on the castle's doorstep. My father was on the telephone pole, reading the repair manual, not even aware of my danger.

I tried to cry out, but still my voice wouldn't work. Just as I reached the second-to-the-last doorway, the fastest of the corpses got a solid grip on the collar of my shirt. I felt my shirt bunching up against my throat. Behind me, I could hear the corpse's bones rattling as it tugged, then I heard my shirt ripping. I half fell forward as a sizable chunk of shirt gave way. The corpse must have fallen backward. The doors slammed shut between us, and there weren't even any corpses in this last, smallest, room—just a tiny entryway, about the size of an elevator. But I staggered, still off balance from the tug that last corpse had given.

And in the instant it cost me to regain my balance, the front door slammed shut in my face.

In the total darkness, I pounded on the door to get my father's attention. But, though behind me I could hear the corpses scratching at the wood and calling out to me, my own fists made no sound. I couldn't make out the corpses' words; still, I figured that was probably all for the best. Somewhere nearby, a bell was ringing, some sort of alarm that kept clanging on and on and on.

At least there're no corpses in here, I thought.

And then I felt something touch my face.

Cobwebs, I thought, and brushed them away.

But then they came back, more solid, more insistent.

I could feel a whimper building in my throat. *If I could only scream,* I thought, *I would wake up.*

At which point, the room began to fill with water.

Over my toes, up my legs, up my torso.

I tried to build the whimper up louder than the scratching or the calling or the bell, to a sound loud enough to wake me.

The water was almost to my chin, past my chin, over my head. But still the cobwebby fingers brushed my face, and still the bell clanged. Despite the water, I opened my mouth for one final attempt at sound.

A scream jerked me awake.

I sat up, my heart pounding. For a second, I thought the scream had been mine, but then there was another one. My eyes focused on Vicki standing in the doorway of my room.

I glanced behind me to make sure that she wasn't screaming because something was about to leap out at me. Reassured, I scrambled out of bed. What if she was sleepwalking? Everybody knows you aren't supposed to wake up sleepwalkers. But Vicki had never sleepwalked before, and it was more likely that she was hurt or frightened. "Vicki," I said—*frightened*, I decided as she threw her arms around me and began to sob—"what's the matter?"

The hall light came on, and Dad called, "What's going on?" I could hear him coming down the hall without waiting for an answer, Mom right behind. From Zach's room next to mine, I heard a thud and an angry mumble: Zach tripping over something on his way to the door.

From Vicki I was getting no sense at all. She had her

face pressed into my stomach and only kept repeating, "The bad lady, the bad lady." She was still saying it when the rest of the family caught up.

"What bad lady?" Dad said, crouching down beside us. "Are you hurt? Ted, what happened?" He wedged his hand between my stomach and her forehead, feeling for a fever.

"She was going to hurt Teddy," Vicki said.

Mom gave me one of those so-you're-behind-all-this looks.

I shook my head to indicate my innocence and ignorance.

"Did you wake us all up for a bad dream?" Zach demanded.

Vicki shook her head. "It wasn't a dream. The bad lady was in my room, and I threw the hammer at her, just like you said, Zach."

Mom turned her look onto Zach, who smiled guiltily, then hunched in his shoulders and tried to look small and innocent.

"And it made her go away," Vicki continued, "but then she floated across the hall to Teddy's room."

Dad said, "If Zach's the one who gave you the hammer, she should have gone after him. *I'll* go after him if that hammer put a dent in the wall."

"This is not funny," Mom told him. "I don't know what kind of stories you two have been telling Vicki—"

"I haven't," Zach protested, at the same time I said, "Not me."

Dad finally pulled Vicki away from me. He gave her a tight hug before picking her up. "I know it seemed real, honey," he said. "But it *was* just a dream."

"It wasn't," Vicki insisted. "I saw her in Teddy's room. She was touching his face."

Zach reeled back in horror, clutching at his heart. "Wow!" he exclaimed. "That *was* dangerous! Good thing you stopped her in time."

"Go to bed," Mom ordered Zach. Then, "Sometimes," she told Vicki, following as Dad began to carry Vicki down the hall back to her room, "when we wake up from an especially real-seeming dream, it takes us a few seconds to stop being confused."

"It wasn't a dream," Vicki said again, as the three of them disappeared into her room.

"We'll leave the hall light on," I heard Dad assure her. "Night-lights keep away both bad dreams and bad ladies."

Zach yawned loudly, scratched his rear end loudly, and returned to his room.

Which left me alone in the hall, wondering why Vicki would dream about the bad lady touching my face at the exact moment I was dreaming about cobwebby fingers touching my face.

On the other hand, I thought with a shudder, maybe I didn't want to work that one out after all....

CHAPTER 5

My Sister Develops an Unreasoning Fear of Susan B. Anthony

THE NEXT DAY WAS Saturday. With the telephone strike, Dad had to work both days of the weekend; for the time being, the only day he had off was Thursday. Mom at least had Saturdays off.

Saturdays Vicki and I go to the Rochester Museum and Science Center for fun-type classes. Zach used to come, too, but now he likes to say he's too smart not to recognize school, however it's disguised. I figure he just doesn't like to get up before noon for fear he'll see his shadow and have to crawl back into his hole for six more weeks. I don't think of it as school. In the past I've taken things like snowshoeing, pottery, "Dinosaur Madness," and "Clownology." At the moment, I was two weeks into a four-week session on magic. Vicki was taking something called "Chipmunks and Squirrels," a nature course that involved, as far as I could see, running around the museum's grounds terrorizing small animals, making leaf rubbings, and stuffing down as many animal crackers as possible.

At breakfast Mom didn't say anything about the night before—as though she was hoping that Vicki and I would each assume it had all been a dream. So everything was the same as usual when she dropped us off in front of the building where they have the classes. I took Vicki to her room (the small kids' rooms are clustered together on the second floor, where their noise won't drive the older kids or the office workers crazy), then I went down to the basement for my class.

On this particular day, we learned a couple rope tricks, a mysteriously-disappearing-then-miraculously-reappearing-coin trick, and how to pull foam-rubber rabbits out of the ears of members of our audience.

I was feeling pretty pleased with myself as I trudged up the eighty or ninety stairs between the basement and the second floor. Everybody else was heading down, of course, to the parking lot and their waiting parents.

By the time I got to the second floor, Vicki was the only one left in the classroom. She was wearing a construction-paper headband decorated with a bird beak and was snarfing down the last crumbs from a box of animal crackers. Her lips were bright grape–Kool-Aid purple.

"Come on," I called to her.

"Wait a minute," Vicki said, tipping the box upside down over her mouth. "There's still some in here."

"Take it with you," I told her. "Mom'll be mad

if she has to park the car and come in looking for us."

Vicki walked down the hall, inhaling into the animal cracker box as though she hadn't eaten in a week.

"Let's take the elevator," I said.

The elevator's so slow, you can run from the second floor all the way down to the basement and back faster than the elevator can make it to the first floor, but Vicki was walking so slow and leaving such a trail of cookie crumbs, I thought it'd be faster.

The only people still in the second-floor hallway were some presenters from "Visiting Old Rochester." "Visiting Old Rochester" is one of those one-day courses that your parents make you take. It's like a local-history career day, going from the Indians to George Eastman founding Kodak, with the teachers dressed in appropriate costumes and telling all about "themselves." Still hanging around were a French fur trapper, a nineteenth-century suffragette, a pioneer child, and Abraham Lincoln, talking together. Not that I have any idea what Abraham Lincoln ever had to do with Rochester, New York.

The elevator finally came and we got in, and I began punching the CLOSE DOOR button simply for something to do, because nothing can speed up that elevator.

But just as the doors slowly began to close, someone called, "Wait up, please," and I stuck my foot out between the doors.

"Thanks." It was the teacher dressed as the suffragette. She set her sign—RIGHTS FOR WOMEN—on the floor and leaned against the wall, waiting for the elevator to start.

Behind me I heard Vicki drop her animal crackers box on the floor. *What a slob,* I thought. I turned to yell at her before the teacher did, and found her pressed up against the back wall, her face white around the Kool-Aid purple of her lips. "It's her," she whispered. She dropped to a crouch, covering her head for protection. I didn't need to ask who "her" was. But how *could* it be her?

The teacher stared at Vicki. "Are you all right, sweetie?" She was young, like most of the teachers at the museum seem to be—probably too young to have kids of her own. Vicki had her face buried in her knees, and she started making a little whimpering sound. The teacher looked at the floor indicator—it still read "2," and it was hard to tell if we were moving yet—then she looked at me. Her expression said, "This little kid isn't going to have some sort of strange fit in here, is she?"

"It's all right, Vicki," I said. "This isn't her. This is just one of the museum teachers. Look at her." *Look at her and reassure me* was what I meant, but Vicki stayed where she was, in her defensive crouch.

The light over the door finally shifted to "1."

I took a firm hold of Vicki's jacket at the shoulder, standing between her and the teacher. Just in case. Not that I'd do much good defending Vicki from a woman who could go through walls and invade dreams.

Vicki continued to whimper.

The teacher continued to look—*I* thought—like she was praying no emergency would occur that she'd have to cope with.

When the doors finally opened, I hauled Vicki to her feet. I was ready to push her past the teacher, but the teacher was out of there even faster. Maybe she thought Vicki was going to throw up on her. She didn't even say anything about the dropped box of cookies. She practically ran into the school office.

I hustled Vicki outdoors.

Mom beeped her horn and we scrambled into the backseat of the car.

"You two look like you've seen a ghost," Mom said as she pulled away from the curb.

I could see into the building, and there was no sign of the teacher lurking there watching us.

Vicki started to cry.

Mom slammed on the brakes and turned around. "Ted, what did you do?"

My fault again. "Vicki thinks she saw the same woman she was dreaming about," I explained.

Mom looked from me to Vicki to me. Finally she said, "Working at the museum?"

I nodded.

Mom bit her lip, considering. "What does she look like?"

"Dark," Vicki said. "Dark, like Marella—but mean."

I nodded. "Dark eyes. Dark hair."

"Dark skin," Vicki added. "Like Bill Cosby, except that he's nice."

That was wrong. "Maybe Italian or Hispanic," I corrected. "Not African American."

"Like Bill Cosby," Vicki insisted.

I shook my head for Mom to see.

"And she was old," Vicki continued, "like Aunt Rose."

Mom said, "Rose would be delighted to hear that." She looked at me.

"About Ms. DiBella's age." Ms. DiBella is my teacher, fresh out of college last year.

"Were you two looking at the same person?" Mom asked.

I remembered how Vicki had been cowering in the corner, not even looking at the woman. "How was she dressed?" I asked Vicki.

"Long black dress." Vicki rubbed her hands over her arms, indicating full-length sleeves. "A black bonnet that tied under her chin."

"It was the costume that was the same," I explained to Mom. "There was a woman on the elevator done up like Susan B. Anthony. But it wasn't the same woman as your ghost, Vicki."

"There is no ghost," Mom said, annoyed with me even though Vicki calmed down instantly.

The car behind us honked.

Mom started driving again. "I'm glad you realize that the museum woman isn't anybody to be afraid of," she said to Vicki. "But there is no such thing as a ghost. And it's very bad of Ted to tell you there is."

"Me?" I said. "How come I always get the blame?"

"I don't want to hear any more about it," Mom said.

But when we got home, she wouldn't let Vicki play outside by herself, and that night she and Dad let Vicki sleep in their room.

CHAPTER 6

I Take Back What I Said about Zach Being the Only Weird One in the Family

EVER SINCE OUR PARENTS started working such long hours, the only time we can all make it to church together "as a family"—"as a family" is one of my father's favorite phrases—is the Saturday evening mass. Sunday mornings, Dad is gone before the rest of us are up, then Mom's got to go to the coffee shop to serve the Sunday brunch crowd. Zach—favorite child that he is—gets to stay home, alone, or he can visit with his friends, so long as he lets Mom know where he is. Vicki and I, of course, are too young to be left on our own, so we get dropped off at the crack of dawn on the doorstep of my aunt and uncle. And then, lucky Vicki and me, we get to go to mass all over again with Uncle Bob and Aunt Rose and Cousin Jackie.

Excuse me; she would prefer *Jaclyn*.

It used to be Jackie, but apparently thirteen-year-olds are too sophisticated for nicknames. Now she insists on Jaclyn. Which is why—whenever her parents aren't there—I try to remember to call her Jac.

Jackie and I used to get along fairly well, although—since she's two years older—she's always had a tendency to boss me around. But now that she's reached the ripe old age of teenagehood, she doesn't want anything to do with me. And she's no more pleased about being stuck with my company on Sundays than I am about being stuck with hers.

"Lisa invited me over," I heard her tell Aunt Rose, just as she'd told her each of the two previous Sundays since we'd started this.

"You have to stay here and entertain your cousin Ted," Aunt Rose answered, her standard reply.

"But you let Vicki go next door and play with Susan," Jackie pointed out, yet again.

"That's different," Aunt Rose said. Ah, family tradition.

And Jackie came back stomping her feet and giving me looks that said, "Why don't you do the family a favor and drop dead?"

I'd just as soon watch basketball on TV with Uncle Bob, even though I'm not crazy about sports, except football when the Buffalo Bills are playing. Come to think of it, I'd just as soon go next door and play with the five-year-olds, but Aunt Rose thinks cousins should like each other.

"Don't just sit around moping," Aunt Rose said, as

she says every time. "Why don't you go to the front room and show Ted your new computer game?"

Jackie sighed—Jackie sighs a lot—but she didn't point out that the game was new at Christmas, three months ago. "Come on, you," she said to me like I was Cinnamon, their dog, and she expected me to heel. And, in fact, Cinnamon did follow, nearly knocking me down in her eagerness to get there first.

Jackie threw herself into the chair in front of the computer and tapped her fingers impatiently on the box of computer disks while I got the hard old piano bench. I noticed that today her fingernails were painted metallic blue with sparkles. Sometimes she uses black nail polish, and sometimes she has each nail a different color. That's the kind of girl Jackie is. She was wearing a black sweatshirt big enough to fit any two thirteen-year-olds, black jeans with holes in the knees, black boots that looked like something the Wicked Witch of the East would wear, a black ponytail holder, and earrings that were miniature dangling handcuffs.

"What do you want to play?" she asked in a bored voice. And then she sighed.

But I wasn't looking at the disks; I was looking at the world map that was tacked up on the wall over the desk. "Oh, shoot," I said.

Jackie's lip curled in disdain. "Chutes and Ladders?"

" 'Shoot,' " I repeated. "As in, 'I was about to use the other word, but I changed my mind at the last minute because I'm talking to a girl.'" And because if my mother even suspected I might use the other word, she'd blame the PG-rated movies I'd gone to and she'd tell me I could only see G movies from now until I left home for college.

Jackie rolled her eyes. "How immature." She sighed again.

"I just remembered my Social Studies Fair project," I explained. "It's due tomorrow, and I've still got to put it together."

"Surely you don't expect that I'm going to help you," she said.

"No," I said. "Jac."

She snarled at me.

I pushed the piano bench back. "I'm going to explain to your mother, then I'm going to borrow your bicycle and go back home to finish the project by myself. I figured you'd be willing to loan me your bicycle if it meant getting rid of me."

"No."

"Come on, Jac—"

"I didn't mean, 'No, you can't use the bike,'" she explained. "I meant, 'No, my mother's never going to let you go by yourself.'"

"I've ridden here and back before," I said. "It's only about forty minutes either way, and no real busy streets."

"Your mother brought you here because she didn't want you home alone."

"She brought me here because she didn't want Vicki home alone and she didn't want me home with Zach." Not that I would have gone back at night, or been willing to sleep there alone. But I figured Sunday afternoon was about as safe a time as there could be.

Jackie was shaking her head. "Mum's responsible for you," she said—she and her friends all call their mothers Mum, as though that's more sophisticated than Mom. Except when Jackie is mad at her mother. Then she calls her Brigadier General Mum, but never to her face. "She'd never let you go all that way on your own. She'd make me go with you."

"Well, why not?" I said. "That'd be better than sitting around here. You could borrow your friend Lisa's bike."

Jackie shook her head.

I figured she was still convinced I was trying to get her help with the project. "If we take Cinnamon along with us—"

Cinnamon recognized her name—it's the only word besides *food* that she does know—and she stood up and began to bark.

I started again, louder. "If we take Cinnamon along with us, then your mother won't make you take her for a walk later. And once we get there, I'll work on Luxembourg on my own. You can play on *our* computer—a whole new set of games."

"Quiet, Cinnamon," Jackie said. Then, to me, she said, "Nah."

I petted Cinnamon to calm her down, and she laid her head in my lap. "Why not?" I asked. "I promise I won't ask you to do a single thing."

Jackie shook her head again.

"Jac," I pleaded.

She looked up at me real quick, angry.

I should have called her Jaclyn, I realized, at least while I was trying to talk her into something.

But she wasn't angry about that. "I don't like your house," she said.

"Well, excuse me," I started.

"Especially now," she continued, before I could think up just the right sarcastic comeback. She quickly glanced away again. "I heard your mother talking to my mother when she dropped you off this morning. She said Vicki's been talking to imaginary friends and having night-mares."

I nodded. "And?" I asked. If Jackie didn't know more than she'd said already, she would have been making the same dropped-on-her-head kind of comments Zach did.

"*And,*" Jackie said, "do these imaginary friends fol-low her to kindergarten or to her other friends' houses? Does she see them anywhere but at your house?"

I figured yesterday at the museum didn't count, since Vicki had been confused by the teacher's costume. "No." I looked at Jackie more carefully, and inspiration hit. "Have you seen them, too?"

Jackie nodded.

It was my turn to sigh. So this had been going on

longer than I thought. "When was the last time you and your parents were over?" I answered my own question. "At Grandma and Granddad's anniversary." We celebrate even though they live in Florida now—a big dinner and then a group phone call where we all try to grab the phone away from one another and shout messages over the voice of whoever actually does have the phone. "Let's see...that was...what?...three, four weeks—"

"No," Jackie said. "Before then."

Something about the way she said it was like cold spiders on the back of my neck. "When?"

Jackie paused to consider. "Eight years ago."

"*What?*"

"It was when I was five. That time when your mother slipped on the ice on your front stoop and broke her leg. Mum was staying over at your place taking care of you and Zach, and I was staying there, too."

That part I remembered, even though I'd been only three.

Jackie continued. "I kept seeing this little girl—and a woman. I never thought they were friends. I knew they were ghosts. And believe me, they scared the— They scared me. Especially the mother."

"The *mother?*" I interrupted. "The bad lady is Marella's mother? Vicki said Marella is afraid of the woman."

Jackie shrugged. "Under the right conditions, *I'm* afraid of *my* mother." She paused. "Well, I assumed they were mother and child, but maybe I was just trying to simplify things. Neither of them ever said anything; I don't think they could talk. The little girl, she just kept making signs like she wanted to go outside to play. But the mother...she'd come at me—real fast—and I could almost feel her pass through my body." Jackie shuddered. "And that angry, hateful look on her face..."

"And you didn't tell anybody?" *How dumb!* I thought.

Jackie smacked me on the arm, which I guess shows that my thought was written on my face. Or maybe it was just frustration, for she said, "Of course I told. I told both my parents. And they yelled at me. They said I was jealous of having to share Mum with you and Zach, and that I was making it up to get attention."

Was she doing that now? "What did they look like?" I asked. *I* had heard the hurried conversation between Mom and Aunt Rose, too, and I knew Mom hadn't gone into any detail at all.

"African American," Jackie said, without having to stop to think.

"Good guess," I acknowledged.

"They were dressed in old-fashioned clothes," she went on. Of course, if they were ghosts, they pretty much had to be.

"How old-fashioned? Bell-bottoms old-fashioned, or animal-skins-and-clubs old-fashioned?"

Jackie looked ready to smack me again. "*Little-House-on-the-Prairie* old-fashioned," she said.

And I figured that was close enough to suffragettes as to be the same thing. "Wow." I sat down on the piano bench. "And do you see them every time you come to our house?"

"No." Jackie shook her head for emphasis. "After a while, they went away. But—and you're an idiot if you never noticed—I've always tried to avoid going to your house just in case they come back. And if I *do* have to go there, I stick real close to..."—she hesitated, then went ahead and said it—"the grown-ups." She leaned back in her chair—I think, trying to judge my reaction. "Have you ever seen them?"

"No."

"Lucky you. But something's got them stirred up again."

"Yeah," I said.

Now, if I could only figure out what.

CHAPTER 7

Luxembourg Suffers a Setback

AFTER THAT CONVERSATION with Jackie, I certainly didn't want to go back to the house, alone or—especially—with her. Since Mom would be picking Vicki and me up around five-thirty, there would be enough time for me to get my project pulled together in the evening if I put my mind to it.

Jackie even ran off a computer-generated map of Luxembourg for me, from an atlas program she has, so that I didn't have to use the *National Geographic* map—and it wouldn't be so obvious that I'd gotten all my information from one source. Then—a real stroke of luck—it turned out she'd had France for her project when she'd been in sixth grade, and France and Luxembourg have the same red, white, and blue stripes on their flags. Except Luxembourg's go from the red stripe at the top to the blue stripe on the bottom, and France's go from the blue stripe on the left to the red one on the right. Jackie had a little French flag she'd gotten when she'd written to the French embassy for information, and she gave it to me to use tipped on its side in the middle of my display so I wouldn't have to draw one.

I was so grateful, as Vicki and I were leaving, I looked Jackie up and down and told her, "You know, Jac, you look like a demented undertaker," and she brightened up.

"Why, thank you, Ted," she said, and both our mothers rolled their eyes.

I wanted to tell Mom what Jackie had said about seeing ghosts in our house long before Vicki started, but I knew she'd explode if I said anything in front of Vicki. So I figured it could wait until the two of us were alone.

Instead, I got the hammer from Vicki's room while she and my mother were arguing about whether it was too late to go out and play in the backyard. I went down into the basement to nail my Luxembourg project together.

As soon as I turned on the light and looked down the stairs, I could tell that something was wrong. "Somebody's been messing with my project," I shouted.

In a much deeper voice, Zach rumbled, "Somebody's been messing with my project." Then he shifted to a tinny falsetto and repeated it again. "Somebody's been messing with my project and has broken it all to bits."

I gave him a dirty look to indicate that if it was him, he was one dead bear, then I ran downstairs.

The pictures, which I had so carefully set out on the piece of paneling, were scattered all over the place, some facedown on the dirt floor, quite a few crumpled as though they'd been stepped on. "Zach!" I hollered, tearing up the stairs with the hammer in my fist, which was—mostly—coincidence.

"Ted!" Mom caught me before I could launch myself at him, which was probably safer for me, after all. "What is your problem?"

"He messed up my project," I yelled.

Zach shook his head in dumb innocence. Well, dumb was normal. "I haven't touched it," he protested.

"Just look," I said, tugging on Mom's arm even though she was trying to get sandwiches together for supper.

She came with me, as did Zach and Vicki.

"Look at this," I said. "Just look at it. As of Friday night, this was all set up and ready to be nailed together."

"I didn't do it," Vicki said.

Zach had grabbed a slice of salami off the kitchen counter, and he shook his head while he swallowed before answering, "And it wasn't me, either." And when Mom gave him a hard look, he added, "Honest. I was at Dom's house all day yesterday and today. You dropped me off and picked me up both times."

"You could have come back," I said. "It's not that far."

"Yeah, right," Zach said. "Like I have nothing better to do."

"Stop bickering." Mom kneeled down and smoothed out the wrinkles from one of the pictures. "Nothing is ruined. It just has to be set up again. It was probably mice."

"Yeah," Zach added, "everybody knows mice don't like Social Studies."

Mom gave him a don't-mess-with-me look. "They were probably running back and forth over the wood and knocked the papers off."

"Yeah," I said, "then a team of them got together and flipped the wood over. I had the good side up."

"Maybe the cockroach did it," Zach said, nodding toward Vicki, "so that her little invisible friend wouldn't do it first."

"Don't call your little sister a cockroach," Mom said.

"No cockroach," Vicki echoed.

Mom finished, "And she wouldn't be strong enough to lift this, anyway. Ted, are you sure?..."

Yeah, I was sure which end I'd had up and that neither Vicki nor mice could have flipped the wood over. And it certainly didn't seem likely that Zach would have gone so far out of his way just to sabotage my homework. I sat down heavily on the bottom step. "I think," I said, "it may have been Vicki's bad lady. I—"

"Ted!" Mom said sharply, at the same time giving Vicki a reassuring hug.

"I was talking to Jackie," I continued. "And she says she used to see Marella and this bad lady, too, when—"

"Oh, jeez!" Zach said, throwing his hands up in the air. "It's contagious!"

"Ted," Mom said, getting to her feet, "that's enough."

"But listen—"

"No more. You were in such a hurry, because you waited till the last second to do this, that you accidentally put the board down the wrong way; then mice ran over the pages, scattering them. I'm sorry you have to do them over again, but that's the way it goes."

No wonder Jackie had given up trying to explain to her parents. *"That's not the way it happened,"* I said, maybe getting a little louder than I should have.

"Don't take that tone with me, young man."

"That's not the way it happened," I repeated with oh-so-careful politeness.

"And don't take *that* tone with me, either," she warned. "Now, do you need help turning that paneling over or not?"

I took a deep breath. "I can do it myself," I said.

Surprisingly, Zach stayed after Mom and Vicki went upstairs, and he helped me get the board right side up. But he didn't say anything; he just shook his head like he was thinking, *It was nice knowing you before you went completely over the edge.* He even got out the staple gun for me, which worked better than the hammer and nails. Then when I was finished, he helped me carry the entire display upstairs. After what had happened, I wasn't going to let it out of my sight until it was safely in Ms. DiBella's possession.

But I was worried. There's a big difference between a ghost who can menace someone's dreams and a ghost who can pick up a solid piece of wood and fling it over.

What *else* could our ghost do?

CHAPTER 8

Here We Go Again

THAT NIGHT, I HAD a dream, which picked up pretty much where the one from Friday night had left off.

I was in the dark, with water over my head. *Don't panic,* I told myself, remembering I was in Luxembourg. *This is a castle. Castles have high ceilings. There'll be air up there.* I kicked off from the bottom, and my head broke the surface of the water. I still couldn't see anything, but I heard voices yelling and, once again, the clanging of a bell.

But the weight of the hammer I was carrying dragged me back under.

My feet settled down to the bottom again, and I kicked off again.

It took longer to reach the top—the water was continuing to rise. In the second or so I had, I heard that the voices were still calling, the bell still ringing, but more distant now, as though we were drifting apart. I gasped in another lungful of air before the water closed over my head. Even so, I was unwilling to let the hammer go.

Once again my feet hit bottom. Once again I launched myself to the top. It seemed to take forever. My lungs were aching, my chest burning. *I'm never going to make it,* I thought.

But I did, momentarily. I caught a glimpse of stars, which sang to me, replacing the voices and the bell, before I began my downward journey again.

Down and down I went. My lungs hurt, my head hurt, my stomach hurt, and I couldn't find the bottom.

And then—just when I thought things couldn't possibly get worse—I felt that cobwebby touch on my face again. I brushed my hand over my eyes to get it away, which I should have done ages ago because suddenly I could see. And I saw that it wasn't cobwebs: It was hair. And the hair was attached to a head, which was attached to a body, a little body—a tiny body—dressed in a long white dress that floated and fluttered in the water. A stray current bobbed the head. Marella, I was sure of it, though I'd never seen her. A sweet-faced little girl no older than Vicki. And obviously dead. Her eyes were closed, her skin was pale gray brown. How incredibly, incredibly sad.

I dropped the hammer, realizing it was Marella I was here to get. I reached out, but she drifted almost out of my range. My hand just barely caught the fabric at the back of her dress. I pulled her close, and I could smell the same rotten-seaweed smell I'd noticed two nights earlier with the corpses. The body twisted around in the water, and it was no longer Marella I held.

It was—obviously—Vicki's bad lady. *Her* eyes were open and full of evil intent. Her dark face was corpse gray, her lips blood red. No wonder she frightened Vicki and made Jackie twitchy. She had the kind of face that if you saw her in a movie, you'd *know* she was the villain. More important, she could breathe underwater, I realized, or she didn't need to breathe at all, and she'd lured me to stay here too long.

Don't breathe in, I told myself, *Don't breathe in.* And the more I said it, the more I knew I had to. *Don't, don't, don't…*

And then I did.

The stars burst in front of my eyes, and the water rushed in, thick as mud, and foul and tasting of old death, and the bad lady watched.

I woke with a start, drenched in sweat and still tasting the water I'd swallowed, which sat in my stomach like a lump of seaweed, reminding me…reminding me…

I fell out of bed, catching my foot in my sheets, and half ran, half staggered down the hall, barely making it to the bathroom before throwing up what felt like the majority of my internal organs.

Somehow Mom was there for the end of it, holding her cool hand against my head. Which was probably all for the best. By then I'd just as soon have crawled into the toilet and flushed myself down.

"What happened?" Mom asked.

Well, we'd both seen what had happened. I guessed she was asking me *why* it had happened. I was in no condition to argue again, so I just shrugged.

"Did you eat something bad at Uncle Bob's and Aunt Rose's?" she insisted.

Why do mothers always ask that? If I knew something was bad, why in the world would I eat it? *Yes, Mom, I ate some two-week-old raw pork that's been sitting on the back porch. It was REAL bad—especially the flies and ants that were all over it.* My stomach was in no mood for sarcasm. "All I had was Uncle Bob's French toast," I whispered. I got a mental image of globs of unmelted butter and thick pools of syrup, and groaned.

"It's probably just the flu," Mom said, handing me a cup of water to rinse the taste of vomit out of my mouth. "Are you feeling better now?"

Well, at least I'd gotten the water a little girl had drowned in out of my stomach. That was a relief no matter how you looked at it. I nodded, and Mom led me back to my room.

She tucked me in. "Want me to stay a bit?" She was probably feeling guilty for having yelled at me earlier.

I figured Vicki, who was still sleeping in my parents' room, had Dad to protect her. I nodded again, and Mom sat on the edge of my bed.

She didn't say anything and I didn't say anything, and before I knew it, I fell asleep.

I WOKE UP WHEN I heard the bus beep. At first I thought I'd dreamed it; but when I opened my eyes, it was much too bright in my room. Then I thought it must be somebody else's bus—but if I was still in bed while *any*body's bus was coming around, I was in trouble.

I ran downstairs, and there was Mom, alone, sponging off the kitchen table.

"You're looking better," she said.

"My bus!" I said.

"Yes, you just missed it."

I sat down in my regular chair. "Why didn't you get me up?"

"You're sick. I already called the school office and told them you wouldn't be in."

I groaned and put my head on the table. Any other day. *Any* other day. "Today's the Social Studies Fair," I protested. "Everybody's going to think I'm faking because I didn't finish my assignment on time." Anytime I did need an extra day, Mom would cheerfully chirp, "You don't look that sick to me."

Now she said, "I'll send in a note tomorrow. Why don't you go back up to bed? I'll bring you some toast and juice."

Tomorrow would be too late, I was sure of it. I thought of my pictures, scattered at the foot of the basement stairs, and I thought of the evil face I'd seen last night, and I realized I'd gotten off easy. A mental image came to me of my Luxembourg display shredded to bits and gnawed on. "Could you bring it in?" I asked.

"What?"

"Luxembourg. Could you bring it in to school so they can set it up? Please?"

She must have still been feeling guilty about yelling at a child who had been obviously sick. Sighing, she said, "All right." She tested my forehead. "Now, how about you? I'm supposed to go in to work at 11:30. Do you want me to call in and stay home with you?"

"No, I'm fine," I assured her. I figured I'd be OK so long as I stayed awake, and being home alone would give me a chance to try something out.

CHAPTER 9

Reach Out and Touch Someone

ALL THINGS CONSIDERED, I decided I preferred being downstairs in the living room rather than in my own room. I brought down my Social Studies display and set it against a wall where I could keep an eye on it—I don't know what Mom made of my sudden devotion to Luxembourg—then I settled in on the couch, in front of the TV. Mom provided me with assorted pillows, an afghan she'd knitted during her arts-and-crafts days, the remote control, a glass of ginger ale—normally reserved for special occasions, but being sick is one of them—and a bucket to throw up in, just in case the ginger ale didn't settle my already perfectly well settled stomach.

"Are you sure you're all right?" she asked, tucking the afghan around me.

"Yes," I told her.

"Are you sure you're all right?" she asked again, before going upstairs to get dressed for work.

"Fine," I told her.

"Are you sure you're all right?" she asked once more, as she put on her jacket to leave for work.

"Great," I told her.

She rested her hand on my forehead despite the fact that she'd already taken my temperature twice that morning and seen that it was normal. She was more convinced I was ill than when I rub the thermometer on the blanket to get the mercury up and roll around moaning. This was worth remembering.

Finally she picked up Luxembourg and left.

As soon as her car pulled out of the driveway, I turned off the TV. If you weren't sick to begin with, daytime TV could get you there.

I called up my grandparents in Florida.

Granddad answered the phone on the second ring.

"Hi, Granddad. It's me, Ted."

"Hi, Ted. How are you doing?" I could hear him turn away from the phone without waiting for an answer and tell Grandma, "It's Ted."

"Hello, Ted," Grandma called out from what was probably the entire length of the apartment.

"Hello, Grandma," I said.

"Ted says, 'Hello.'" Granddad passed it on to her. To me he said, "Grandma can't come to the phone right now. She's elbow deep in potting soil. She picked this morning to repot every single plant in the place."

"That's not true," Grandma said. "I never touched the rubber tree."

"So," Granddad said, "you kids up there in New York got another day off from school? When I went to school, *we went to school*. It seems like kids today have a day off every week."

"Actually I'm home with the flu," I said, which was the simplest explanation.

"Oh, that's too bad." Again his voice faded. "He says he has the flu."

It was Grandma's turn. "Poor sweetie."

"Actually I'm feeling all better now," I told them. "I just wanted to ask you some questions about the house."

"Sure," Granddad said. "Is this some sort of school project—because of the old Erie Canal bed out back?"

"No," I said real quick. But not quick enough.

Grandma had heard the magic words. I could hear her start singing, as she always does at the mention of the Erie Canal. "'Looooow bridge, everybody down. Looooow bridge, for we're coming to a town.'" She got louder, as she must have moved in closer to the phone. "'Oh, you'll always know your neighbor, you'll always know your pal, if you've ever navigated on the Erie Canal.'"

I moved the phone back to my ear. "Real nice, Grandma," I told her. It wasn't as bad as it could have been. At least this time there weren't nonfamily members present.

Granddad said, "We're safe. She's gone back to the porch again." She answered back something I couldn't hear, then Granddad continued, "So, what's your question?"

"Did anybody ever die in our house?"

There was a long pause, then Granddad and I both spoke at once. I asked, "Like, especially, a little girl?" as Granddad asked, "What kind of school project is this?"

"It's not exactly a school project," I admitted. "I'm just wondering, you know, since the house is so old, if it could be, like, sort of, haunted."

"Not that I ever heard of," Granddad said. "Let's see...Did anybody die?" Grandma asked something, and he told her, "No, he wants to know if anybody ever died in the house." To me he said, "You're asking about children, did you say? Girls? Actually there haven't been that many girls in the family. Like about how old?"

I didn't want to say "Vicki's age," for fear they'd think there was something wrong with her my parents hadn't told them. "Please just tell me about the house."

"Well, it was built by old Theodore Beatson and his wife, Winifred, in the 1840s. Winifred lost three or four babies in childbirth, I believe. I don't know if any of them were girls. Is that what you need?"

"I don't think so," I said. Marella was very definitely not a baby. And this certainly didn't explain the woman Jackie took to be Marella's mother.

"Let's see if I can remember this," Granddad said. "The two children who survived were Rebekka and Jacob. Do you need the dates?"

"No," I told him. "You don't have to be that exact."

"Theodore died in the Civil War—no famous battle, he caught dysentery in the Union camp. Jacob went to war, too, but only right in time for the end. Afterward he got married and moved to Watertown. Meanwhile Rebekka stayed at home to care for her mother, who was always sickly after all those hard pregnancies and dead babies. Winifred died a few years after the war—probably at the house itself."

But she would have been an old lady by then, I thought. And she probably wasn't African American, unless there was something about our family nobody was telling me.

Granddad continued, "The house went to Rebekka, who stayed a spinster all her life. Toward the end, her brother, Jacob, and his wife—Eudora, I think it was—moved in with her."

"Did Jacob and Eudora have any kids?" I asked to get him back on track.

"Of course they did," Granddad said. "Where do you think we come from? But they were all grown up by the time Jacob and Eudora moved back to Rochester. The house went to the oldest, my father's brother—the black sheep of the family, my crazy uncle Josiah—when their parents died."

"Black sheep" made my heart skip a beat before I remembered that it meant somebody nobody wanted to admit being related to. "Josiah's the one who made the house into a tavern," I said, remembering this part.

Grandma must have abandoned the repotting and been sharing the phone with Granddad. Her voice chirped into the receiver, "And not a nice one."

Granddad repeated, as though Grandma's volume hadn't nearly punctured my eardrum, "Grandma says, 'And not a nice one.' He kept it going even during Prohibition. Gin and loose women."

I heard Grandma hiss at him that I was too young for him to be talking to me about loose women. "Did he have any kids?" I asked.

"Nope," Granddad said. "That's why the house came to me, in 1947."

Grandma called into the phone, "And what a mess it was."

"I thought you were repotting," Granddad scolded her. To me, he said, "And we, of course, only had boys: your father, your uncle Bob, and your uncle Steve. I suppose one of the tavern girls could have died. Those were pretty rough times. *What?*" That last was apparently directed to Grandma, who was scolding him in the background again.

None of this was any help.

"OK," I said. "Well, thanks a lot."

"Ted?" Grandma had obviously wrested the phone from Granddad. "What exactly is this school project?"

"Well, it's not really a school project," I started.

"Because," Grandma continued, "if you need to write about something interesting that happened in your house, you could write about the secret room."

A tingle of excitement started all over me, but I told myself it was probably nothing. "What secret room? You mean down in the basement?" There are several little rooms down there—root cellars, and places for shelves and shelves of canned food, needed in the days before refrigerators and easy shopping trips to the supermarket. I'd explored all of them before I was old enough to go to school.

But, "No," Grandma said. "This was a tiny room we found under the kitchen when we ripped up the kitchen floor—under the kitchen, but over the basement."

This was totally new to me.

Grandma went on. "We had no idea it was there, just an empty space, oh, maybe as big as the new powder room but not nearly as tall. And there wasn't even a trapdoor to get down there, though that was probably covered over when Josiah turned the place into a tavern. We wouldn't have found it except that we ripped up the subflooring when we put in the gas furnace. It got sealed back up again when we finished the floor."

"Was there..."—I swallowed hard—"anybody buried in there?"

Grandma laughed at me. "No," she said. "No bodies. The only thing we found was an old journal— Winifred's?" She and Granddad had a hasty discussion. "Winifred's or Rebekka's, we can't remember. We read it at the time, and I remember it had something to do with the Underground Railroad."

"The Underground Railroad?" I squeaked.

Grandma, who doesn't think any more highly of the New York State school system than Granddad does, figured I didn't know what she was talking about. "Harriet Tubman," she said. "Frederick Douglass. Runaway slaves."

"In our house?" I was impressed. *That has to be it*, I thought, getting a mental picture of Vicki's bad lady. A runaway slave who'd died and who held me and Vicki, as white kids, responsible. Well, maybe not. That left too many questions unanswered—like, How come she'd haunted Jackie and Vicki but not Zach and me? and What about all those years in between dying and now?—but at least it was a beginning. "You didn't put the journal back in the room when you sealed it up, did you?" I asked.

"No," Grandma said. "We put in some newspapers and magazines for somebody else to find, someday—"

"You also left my measuring tape in there," Granddad complained.

"You should have moved it when I told you to," Grandma snapped. "Now what did we do with the journal?"

"Beats me," Granddad said.

"I think it's in the attic," Grandma told me. "We thought maybe one of our boys might want to bring it into school one day, so we left it out. I don't think any of them ever did, so it's nice that you will. I think it's in the attic."

If it was in the attic, I knew exactly where it had to

be: in a trunk full of stuff my mother had gathered together that was in the house before she and Dad got married. "Thank you, thank you, thank you," I said.

"You're welcome," Grandma said. "Good luck on your school project."

"It's not—" I started.

"Say good-bye, Floyd," she told Granddad.

"Bye-bye," Granddad said.

"Bye-bye," I answered.

CHAPTER 10

I Take a Trip to the Attic

I WASN'T EVEN THINKING scary thoughts as I put my hand on the doorknob of the door to the attic stairs. I was thinking of the ghosts of Marella and her mother more as a puzzle that was about to be solved than as spooky business.

But then I put my hand on the doorknob.

There was a loud bang and the door shook, as though someone on the attic side had taken a flying leap off the top stair and crashed into the door.

I took a quick step back.

The doorknob moved and rattled.

I took another step back.

The big brass key—which nobody ever uses to lock the door and which is always in the lock because, my mother points out, if we ever took it out, we'd never find it again—the key wiggled, then flew out of the lock, landing near my feet.

On the other hand, I told myself, as I quickly put more distance between the key and my feet, *this can probably wait until Zach or Mom or Dad gets home.*

The fact that they didn't believe in ghosts wasn't important. I could tell them that I'd talked to Grandma about the journal and didn't want to mess around with their stuff.

Which didn't sound like me at all—I knew any one of them would demand to know what I was really up to.

Plus, it'd never work with Zach. He'd tell me to get the journal myself.

Which left Mom or Dad. Was it fair to send someone all unsuspecting up against a ghost who could pound doors and throw keys? Yet, if I tried to warn them the ghost was up there, that would distract them while they yelled at me that there wasn't any such thing as a ghost. *Then* they'd tell me to get it myself.

Besides, the ghost obviously didn't want me up in the attic. Why not? I'd been up there Saturday afternoon looking for rope to show off the magic rope tricks I'd learned at the museum. Why had the ghost let me up then but not now? The only answer was that the ghost had been eavesdropping. She'd heard Grandma tell me about the journal, and she didn't want me seeing it.

Which meant I absolutely *had* to get it now because, if I waited for my parents, chances were the journal would end up in even worse shape than how I'd found my Luxembourg project.

I stood with my back against the hallway wall, watching the key just sitting there on the floor and feeling my heart rate slow down to about five beats per second or so.

All right, I told myself, still just standing there. *All right.*

I was looking for some excuse to stay just where I was, but nothing came to me.

All right.

I pushed myself away from the wall, and the key started to move. For a second I froze.

The ghost seemed to be having a difficult time— which was good. Which meant she wasn't as capable of handling solid objects as I had feared. Which I should have found reassuring.

But then slowly, steadily, the key started sliding across the rug, away from me. Toward the door. Toward the crack under the door. She'd locked the door, I realized, and now she was about to put the key beyond my reach.

I lunged, throwing myself on the key like one of the Buffalo Bills sacking somebody else's quarterback.

I thought I'd feel something at least semisolid, but there was nothing, not even the sense of cold I'd expected, like air released from a long-sealed coffin. For a second I wondered if I'd missed. I reached under myself, in the vicinity of my chest, which was where I estimated the key should be, and there it was.

Clutching the key tightly, just in case she tried to get it away from me, I sat up.

Nothing.

I'll just sit here for a couple hours and catch my breath, I thought.

But if she wasn't here, she was probably up in the attic, searching for the journal.

So, against my better judgment, I got up, unlocked the door, then tucked the key into my pocket. Unless this ghost was a pickpocket, she wouldn't be locking me in.

I opened the door.

Something slammed it shut again, in my face.

Taking a steadying breath and getting my foot ready, I opened the door again.

Nothing.

Or, at least, nothing I felt.

I reached up and tugged on the string that switches on the light over the stairs.

The light came on.

A second later it turned off.

I had taken only one step up. I turned back and tugged the string again, this time not letting go.

The light came on.

"There," I said out loud for the ghost to hear.

The lightbulb exploded.

This was getting worse and worse, but there was nothing I could do. I let go of the string and ran up the stairs. The attic is one gigantic room, with two big round windows at the front and the back of the house and one short but wide one on the right-hand side, so I didn't really need the light, anyway.

Upstairs was cold and dusty. Clothes bags hung on racks, always there to hold clothes from whatever season it wasn't. Most of our outgrown clothes went to the Salvation Army, but there were boxes that held "special" clothes—the baptism gown all three of us had worn, my First Communion suit (Zach's had been loaned to Scott Bickham, our next-door neighbor, who'd moved away without returning it), souvenir T-shirts we'd gotten on various vacations—and the duffel bag containing Dad's stuff from his years in the Marine Reserves.

As I walked past the boxes of clothes, there was a crash behind me. I whirled around and saw that one of the boxes from the top of the pile had fallen to the floor.

Behind me—the direction I *had* been going—there was another thud. Again I turned. It was another box, this one from the section where Mom saved every single drawing and test and homework assignment from our years in school. (Someday, if we survived long enough, Luxembourg would be up here, too.)

Yet another box of clothes hit the floor. I forced myself not to turn around. "Enough nonsense," I said, not sounding nearly as stern as Ms. DiBella can manage.

There was a flapping noise at the side window, like

bat wings smacking frantically against the glass. That got me to look, even though I know bats don't move around in the daylight.

Nothing.

I was trying hard not to breathe like I was going into a panic, even though I was going into a panic.

There were old rolled-up rugs here, baby furniture we were holding onto just in case Uncle Steve ever settled down and started a family, boxes of decorations from Easter and Valentine's Day and Thanksgiving and Christmas, and that holiday that comes before Thanksgiving that I didn't even want to think about at this particular moment, and—

Something brushed against my ankle.

I shuddered but forced myself not to look. *Probably a spider,* I told myself, *and I'm not afraid of spiders.* Or a hairy dustbunny. Or...

It doesn't make any difference, I told myself. *Just keep walking.*

I walked past all the old lamps and chairs and general stuff that a family keeps, things that are too old-fashioned or too ugly to use but too good to throw away, until there, under the far window, I spied the trunk I had always thought looked like a treasure chest, the one that had held my grandparents' things when they had been young and just married and had honeymooned in Europe years and years and years ago.

Kneeling down in the dust in front of the trunk, I pushed up the lid.

And nearly lost my fingers as it slammed back down again.

"Knock it off, you," I said, my confidence inching upward since she seemed, after all, incapable of getting a good solid hold on me.

I opened the trunk again.

There were mostly books in there; Mom is physically incapable of getting rid of books. And these weren't even hers. There were schoolbooks from the 1960s with my father's and my uncles' names written in them; books with real exciting names, like *The Red Book of Fairy Tales* and *The Blue Book of Fairy Tales*; newspapers from when Alan Shepard became the first American man in space and from the day John Kennedy was shot; my grandparents' 1950 passports; a red leather book, which I thought might be what I was looking for but it turned out to be a sign-in book from the funeral parlor for my great-grandmother Caroline.

So far all I'd done was rummage through the trunk. What I needed to do was unpack it, take things out to get to the lower layers. I'd just decided that, when I realized what I was doing: While I used my right hand to sort through the mess, my left hand had been holding back a little book with a cracked black leather cover.

I opened the book. Lines and lines of handwritten words, close together but still somehow spidery. I turned one thick yellow page and the next, and there in the middle of the page, the names Rebekka and Jacob leaped out at me. The children of Theodore and Winifred

Beatson. One more page, and there at the top was the date May 5, 1851.

I gave a sigh of relief.

Behind me someone screamed.

For a second I thought it was Vicki; it was a little girl's voice, there was no question. But Vicki wasn't there. Nobody was. The scream went on and on and on.

And then, in the dust on the floor, I could see footprints. Two sets of footprints. One, little-kid-sized. The other, an adult. No feet, no shimmer of ghostly presence. No sound of scuffling. Just the visible footprints. And the scream. Angry and frightened and very young. "No," she cried, and I remembered Vicki saying, "She can talk if she has to, but it's hard." "No, Mamma. No! No! NO!"

The adult was moving backward, apparently dragging the child away from me.

I jumped to my feet. "Stop it!" I yelled. "Leave her alone! What are you doing?"

I followed the footprints—much good that I could do. Five steps, six, seven.

And then the scream cut off like someone had hit a mute button. There was no step number eight. The footprints stopped in the middle of the floor.

I swiped at the empty space with Winifred's journal.

Not that I would have felt anything, even if Marella and the bad lady *were* still there.

But somehow, I had the feeling they weren't.

CHAPTER 11

Great-Great-Grandmother Winifred Gets an Unexpected Visitor

I HALF EXPECTED to find the attic door closed and barricaded, but it was open, just the way I'd left it. Going down the stairs, I clutched the handrail, just in case the ghost decided to trip me or give a little shove from behind. No sign of her.

Downstairs looked totally normal, too. I settled myself onto the couch. The book smelled hot and dusty. My hands shook as I opened it to a random page, trusting that fate would direct me to the right passage.

The words *Marella, ghost,* and *dead* did not leap out at me.

I searched more closely.

The script was so fancy, it was hard to read, and it went from the very top of the yellowed page to the very bottom and from margin to margin, with no space between lines. Also, Great-Great-Grandmother Winifred or her pen had had serious problems with blots. For a while I thought that Winifred was a really bad speller, but then I realized that what looked like long, tipping-over *f*s were really *s*s. Too bad they didn't have computers and printers back then, or, at least, typewriters. I struggled through the whole page, and all Winifred talked about was the weather (miserable) and how she was embroidering some hand towels for a charity bazaar at the church and how the woman who ran the bazaar— Leona something-or-other-that-I-couldn't-make-out— was a gossip with what Winifred called a "vicious tongue."

I skipped ahead a few pages, thinking maybe somebody killed off this Leona woman. But apparently not.

OK, so fate hadn't directed my hands to open the book at that particular spot. I leafed through the book, searching for when Vicki had first mentioned seeing Marella—mid-March—in case she had appeared because that day was the anniversary of her death. But I really didn't have much confidence in that idea. From 1851 to now wasn't a nice round number like one year, or one hundred years, or a thousand years: important numbers, significant anniversaries that might drag ghosts out of their graves.

Still, I read over the entries from around that time, just in case. More talk about the weather, and a complaint that the material she had bought for Rebekka's new dress had faded already.

Next I checked the date of Vicki's birthday, July 15, in case the ghosts were somehow tied to that, but there wasn't even an entry for that day; and the following day, Winifred just wrote—in especially illegible handwriting—that her rheumatism was so bad she could hardly move. That seemed to pretty well kill the ghosts-looking-at-the-calendar theory.

So I started from the beginning.

I didn't read every single passage, but I did at least skim every page.

The journal started in November, 1850, which was long before Great-Uncle Josiah sold off the greater portion of the land to become a tavern owner rather than be a farmer. This was while the Erie Canal still ran through our backyard, before sections of it fell into disrepair and were rerouted years later. So a lot of Winifred's entries talked about canal traffic and day-to-day events on a farm, and about her husband, Theodore, and their children, Rebekka and Jacob. Winifred didn't write about politics or runaway slaves or cleaning secret rooms. And she would have written about it if she'd done it. She wrote about *every*thing. There were lots of entries that said things like:

Today I hung all the rugs on the line and beat them vigorously since this will probably be the last chance I shall have to do so before the weather becomes truly inclement. I noticed that the small braided rug from the parlor had a few broken stitches, so I promptly mended it lest someone catch a heel.

I mean, Real Exciting Stuff.

But then, suddenly, February 10, Winifred caught my attention:

It is nine o'clock of the evening, and the children are asleep, and Theodore, if not asleep, is in bed also, and all is quiet, and still when I place my hand over my heart I can feel the rapid hammering of it against my ribs.

Bitsy, who has always sought out the most inconvenient places to lay her eggs, has most recently been nesting in the barn loft. This morning, when I went up there to look for eggs, I found a man, who had evidently entered our barn during the night and crawled into the straw for warmth. He was half covered with straw and all curled up tight in a ball so that, actually, my first impression was that it might be a child. At first I thought he must be dead, for he lay so still, and he was wearing nothing but rags despite the snow on the ground. I gave a cry of surprise and the man leaped to his feet, and that was when I saw that he was a full-grown man and a Negro, at that.

The only thing that kept me from calling out for help immediately was that the baling fork was ready at hand, and I placed it between us.

"Canada?" the man asked. He had so thick an accent and his speech was so slurred from cold and sleep

that I did not truly understand until after he repeated himself, but still I heard the tone of hope in his voice. "Do this be Canada?" he asked.

"No," I said, "this is our barn loft."

The look of hope became one of fear, despite that he loomed two feet taller than me, or at least he would have except that he was hunched over trying to keep warm. Our frosty breaths hung in the air between us.

He asked, "Abolitionist?"

"No," I said, and he sank, exhausted and defeated, to the floor. He wrapped his arms around himself and let his gaze also fall to the floor, as though he was saying, "Take me. I am too tired to try anymore."

I stood there in the barn loft thinking that he was a desperate fugitive and that I endangered my life not to call out to Theodore. Perhaps as soon as I turned my back he would lunge at me.

But he did not look capable of lunging. He did not look capable of walking. He looked cold and starving and frightened.

Still, I backed away from him rather than turning from him, and I kept the baling fork up for as long as I could till I reached the ladder going to the lower level.

"Stay there," I said, because he had not yet looked up at me and he might not even be aware that I was leaving. "Don't come near me."

At my words, he did look up, the skin of his face darker than any I'd ever seen this close up, but his eyes the same as anybody else's.

Back in the house, I decided that I could cause no hurt by making the man some food. Even if the slave catchers had followed him and were about to descend on our house, he had to eat before they brought him back South to whatever place it was he'd run away from. I also decided that Theodore had enough old shirts that surely one could be spared. And if the Negro man should happen to wander away while I prepared food and sought clothing for him, so much the better.

But as soon as I walked in the door, I realized I was still holding the baling fork. Theodore, who'd been slicing the breakfast bread, looked up at me with concern and shooed the children away.

I worked at preparing a sandwich with thick slices of cold pork so that the children would not guess that we were talking about something we didn't want them to hear, which would fetch them underfoot faster than anything else in the world. "There is a runaway Negro slave in our barn loft," I whispered.

Theodore sighed. He said, "He was probably looking for the Stearnses' farmstead."

The Stearns are Quakers and everybody knows Quakers are all abolitionists.

I said, "He was looking for Canada."

"Any sign of federal marshals or slave catchers?" Theodore asked. I shook my head, and he said, "One of us must ride out to fetch them."

"I know," I said.

"Otherwise," he pointed out, "with that new law, we

are responsible. We could face a thousand-dollar fine. Building this house cost less than a thousand dollars."

"A thousand dollars is a great deal of money," I agreed.

"And six months in jail," Theodore said.

"Six months is a long time," I agreed. I pulled his heavy work shirt off the hook by the door and slung it over Theodore's arm. I handed him the sandwich. "Perhaps, if we're lucky, he has gone," I said.

But he wasn't gone.

And when Theodore saw that the Negro man's shoes were entirely worn through so that he'd been walking in the snow with what were essentially bare feet, he invited him into the house.

And when the man took off his ragged shirt to replace it with Theodore's shirt and we saw the whip scars, some discolored, some with the skin raised like permanent welts on his back, we told him he could spend the day, and at night we would put him in the cart and drive him to the Stearnses' farm.

All day long we waited for the slave catchers to come and catch us at what we were doing.

They came just as I was putting supper on the table.

Rebekka, who is very responsible for eight years old, had been staying in the front room so that she could catch an early glimpse and warn us of any visitors. She came running into the kitchen shouting, "Three men on horses."

At that time the runaway Negro was in the root

cellar, where they would be sure to find him if they forced their way in and searched the house.

Theodore told Rebekka, "Take Jacob downstairs and choose some fine juicy apples for supper." Rebekka nodded solemnly, knowing what was behind the words. To Jacob, Theodore said, "Do you think you can help your sister?" because four years old is too young to understand, and we knew Jacob would tell our new visitors about the black-skinned visitor who was also here today. Fortunately, Jacob was eager to help Rebekka.

The men who came were the slave owner and two professional slave catchers. The owner said he was looking for his runaway Nigro—that was how he said it, "Nigro." "A prime field slave," he said, "but ungrateful and uppity." I thought of the quiet dignity of the Negro man compared to the red-faced bluster of these three. It was easy to lie to them, to say we had seen nothing of any Negroes. They didn't demand to search the house and left shortly after arriving.

After supper we loaded the former slave onto our cart and covered him with old flour sacks. By that time we had given him two of Theodore's shirts, a blanket, a new pair of shoes, and all the food that would fit into his pockets.

I worried and worried while Theodore took him to the Stearnses' farm. It seemed he was gone forever, but when he came back, he said everything had gone smoothly. He had seen no one on the way and had tapped quietly on the door only after making sure there was no sign of the slave catchers. He said Thomas Stearns seemed surprised at the late-evening visit, but once Theodore told him we'd had a surprise visitor in our barn, he grasped the situation immediately. "Let him come in," Theodore said he said, "and God be with thee for thy kindness."

It was a foolish risk, we both agreed, but the matter that most tugs at my conscience is, I never thought to ask the Negro man his name.

CHAPTER 12

A Friend, with Friends

I REALIZED I'D BEEN reading all in a rush. My heart was pounding and my hands were sweaty. *Sentimental jerk,* I told myself, *to get so caught up in things that happened a hundred and fifty years ago.* Everybody involved was long dead. The passage had explained a lot—such as that Grandma's secret room must have been added later or they wouldn't have needed to hide the runaway in the root cellar. But the passage did not explain what I needed to know.

I flipped through the next pages, looking for something that would help me, but all the while I was wondering, *Did he make it to Canada? He must have,* I thought; he was so close. It takes us a little more than an hour's drive (two, if Dad's behind the wheel rather than Mom), heading west toward Buffalo, then over one of the three or four bridges at Niagara Falls.

If those bridges were up in the 1800s.

And, of course, it would be slower without cars and expressways.

Not to mention with slave catchers breathing down your neck.

I looked for more, for an acknowledgment from their Quaker neighbors that they'd safely delivered the man to Canada or had received word that he'd arrived safely.

But there was nothing more about him.

Except, maybe, that in a couple of places—before an entry, or after one and having nothing to do with anything—Winifred wrote things like:

All worrying does is pass the time.

Then, on June 23, in the middle of complaining that it had rained every day for the past two weeks and talking about a shopping trip, Winifred mentioned the neighbors again:

I saw Naomi Stearns at the notions counter, where I was looking for new brass buttons for Jacob's jacket. Naomi smiled and nodded but had not a word for me until I was leaving, having found nothing to my liking. Then, just as I passed her, she turned and, doing so, knocked over with her elbow a display of lace and ribbons from the counter. "Oh my, how clumsy!" she said, and putting her bag on the counter so that she could more easily pick up the spools of ribbon, she knocked a box containing packages of pins and needles off the opposite side of the counter.

Never having seen Naomi Stearns be anything less than graceful, I estimated all of this was intentional, so I stooped down to help her fetch up the rolling spools, leaving Mr. Willoughby on the far side of the counter to scramble after the pins.

Naomi whispered to me, "Federal marshals are watching my husband and me."

"Yes?" I said, making pretense that I did not understand, though I feared I did. Already I was certain I did not want to become involved. Through the open doorway of the store, I could see a man who was unfamiliar to me loitering in the doorways across the street, watching us while pretending not to, though anyone with any sense at all would go in out of the rain.

Naomi said, "There is a shipment of black wool being sent here from North Carolina."

I started to shake my head, but Naomi clutched my wrist.

"Two bales of wool," she said. "One ewe's wool, the other from a tiny lamb."

If this was the secret language of those who helped slaves escape, it certainly wasn't difficult to decipher. Two slaves, she was telling me, a woman and a child.

"They had to be shipped from their previous location, and now they cannot come to our house. Winifred, think thee how cold and wet it has been. They have been outdoors for the past two days."

My intent was to say no, but I found my tongue asking, "How long?"

"Overnight," she answered. "Tomorrow after sunset, there will be a boat on the canal. Show a lantern and they will come. Identify thyself as a friend, with friends. The Federal marshals have no reason to suspect thee, so all will be perfectly safe."

"I must discuss this with my husband," I said, handing her the last of the rolls of ribbon.

Naomi bit her lip. "What is he like to say?"

"Yes," I admitted. "Likely he will say yes."

"Many thanks," Naomi said out loud. "It is very kind of thee to help me in my clumsiness." She stood and began to apologize to Mr. Willoughby and she did not look at me again. I left the store and knew enough not to look behind me to see if the man across the street watched me or Naomi.

Theodore, of course, said yes.

A woman and a child. It had to be our two ghosts, Marella and her mother. I was about to find out what had happened. I turned the page. The next entry simply said:

A cold nasty day. A dismal beginning to July.

July?

I checked the date over the entry. July 1, 1851. I backed up a page. The previous entry, the day Winifred met Naomi Stearns and agreed to take in the slaves, was June 23.

I ran my finger along the binding to see if pages had been ripped out. There were no pages missing, and when I thought about it, there couldn't have been. The previous day's entry had ended just about at the bottom of the right-hand page, and the next one started in on the same sheet, at the top of the left-hand page. Winifred—who wrote every single day, except when her rheumatism was too bad, even when all she had to say was that she had dusted the parlor or Theodore had painted the front step—had skipped seven and a half days and wasted the next.

My eyes strayed farther down the page, to the next entry, which began:

The worst possible thing in the world has happened.

Since my left hand holding the book was suddenly shaking, I used my right hand to keep my place.

CHAPTER 13

The Worst Possible Thing

July 2, 1851

The worst possible thing in the world has happened. I keep returning to it over and over again in my mind, thinking, What could I have done to prevent it, what did I do wrong? An occurrence so violent and bizarre, it seems an act of God, a punishment for some evil. And yet, how could such a punishment be directed against those who so obviously trusted in Him and had suffered so much? Was it our sin—mine and Theodore's—to have presumed too much, to have arrogantly placed trust in our own abilities?

July 3, 1851

I have tried, several times these past nine days, to set pen to paper. Theodore says I have become silent and bitter. I have seen enough of silent and bitter old women that I do not want to become one. I need to try harder, I need to get the words and the feelings out, I need to start at the beginning.

There was a quiet knock at our door during our supper that Monday night. It was one of the Stearns children. They have so many I cannot tell them one from the other, but this was one of the boys, of about ten or eleven years, and he had with him a tall Negress carrying a child. They were both wearing clothes more appropriate for high summer than for a rainy Rochester night. Someone, possibly the Stearnses', had given them two rough-woven blankets, but the mother had them both wrapped around her child and none for herself.

The Stearns boy said he must get home before the watchers became suspicious that he was gone so long and in the wet, and reminded us, before he left, to hang a lantern tomorrow evening on the old elm tree that leans over the canal for those on the canal boat to see.

The first thing I did was to ask their names. The Negress said her name was Adah, and the child, who was five years old, which would make her one year older than Jacob, was Marella.

Before we had done more than to sit them down at the table and put warm food in front of them, Jacob pointed out that they both spoke much more clearly than the Negro we helped four months ago. I was much embarrassed, but Adah said that she and her daughter were not field hands but both worked at the big house,

by which I took her to mean at the home of the plantation owner himself. I did not say what I was thinking,
which was that five years old was too young for
Marella to be working anywhere, nor did I mention that
Marella was several shades lighter in skin than her
mother, which I suspected was indication that Adah was
required to do more than cook and clean at the big
house.

Over the rest of that evening and the next day, Adah
and I talked a great deal. God had blessed her, she insisted, with a kind master. She said this despite the fact
that her arms were as big around as Theodore's from
lifting and carrying and other heavy work. And despite
the fact that, though Adah had a husband, Marella was,
as I had guessed, the master's daughter. Adah's husband
had been gentle and loving to the child, but he had been
sold, as Adah put it, downriver. Adah did not blame her
master for this because the husband had been caught
learning to read, which is illegal. The man who was
teaching him, a free Negro carpenter, had been killed.

I thought it was having her husband sent away
from her and to the deep South which had caused Adah
to risk her life for freedom for herself and her daughter,
but, in truth, the matter that had decided her was that
the master was getting married. Other slaves had
warned her that Marella looked too much like the master for the new wife to tolerate. She would be sent out to
the fields, or she might be sold to the owner of a nearby

plantation who had a reputation for being very fond of
young mulatto girls, the younger the better.

I am still too angry to even think about that.

I stopped reading, started again, then figured it
might be important, so I went to the dictionary and
looked up *mulatto.* The dictionary said: "A person of
mixed Caucasian and Negro ancestry," which I'd already
caught on to. I pretty much figured I knew what the rest
of it meant, too. And I figured I was probably as angry
about it as Winifred. Back to the journal:

I had been afraid that the hours would drag like days
while we hid these poor fugitives from the slave catch-
ers, that I would be so nervous about the possibility of
discovery that time would not even seem to move for-
ward. But once they were actually under our roof, it was
not as I had expected. Talking to Adah was like talking
to a friend from a different country. I say a different
country because much of how she described her life
seemed so foreign to what I have ever known, and I say
friend because I immediately admired her courage, her
steadfast devotion to God and her child, her ability to
think well of people despite all she had been through,
which would have turned me bitter.

Bitter. As I write down that word I remember that I
have turned bitter.

Adah was not a friend for all I have said she seemed

one. She was a piece of runaway property pursued by her owner and by the law.

Late in the afternoon of Tuesday, June 24, a man came to our door saying he had reason to believe we were harboring a runaway slave.

No, Theodore said, while Adah and her child and I and my children sat still and quiet in the downstairs parlor, where the drapes were drawn shut, not daring to breathe.

The man demanded to search our house.

"I do not know you," Theodore said. "Why should I let you come in my house? You may well be a thief, for all I know."

The man showed him a paper, which identified him as a professional slave catcher.

Theodore said, "Come back with a Federal marshal, and I will let you in."

"Nigger lover," the man called him.

"No nigger lovers here," Theodore said, and quietly shut the door in his face.

I stopped, shocked that my great-great-grandfather would use that word and that my great-great-grandmother would repeat it. In October we'd read part of *Huckleberry Finn,* and everybody knows the author, Mark Twain, used that same word. But Ms. DiBella said it was too offensive to say out loud, so she always substituted *African American* or *person of color* instead. I was amazed that Winifred and Theodore, whom I'd been thinking of as the good guys, could be so offensive.

I returned my attention to the journal.

We knew that the man could not be back before nightfall, but we had no safe place to hide Adah and her child. I had already given Adah an old dress of mine, having finally admitted to myself that I will never be that slender again. Fortunately, the sleeves were full, to cover her muscular arms; but for all that, Adah was a thin woman, so the dress did fit, though I needed to sew a long strip of black ruffle to the bottom hem, else the dress ended several inches above her ankles. And for sweet little Marella, we found one of Rebekka's dresses, a white one from when she was hardly more than a baby, for Marella, also, was very thin.

And then, as the sky grew darker, we sent them out into the cold and wet night.

The canal being a good two hundred feet back from the house, and the yard having fewer than a dozen trees to hide behind, and those far between, we could not risk Adah and Marella waiting for the slave catcher to return and then making their way to the canal. They had to wait by the bank of the canal, the lantern we'd given them shuttered until they heard the approach of a boat, lest they attract the attention of those who would return them to their kind master.

Such a terrible night, I thought, as the rain lashed at the windows and my ears picked up the rumbling of thunder coming in from the west. Surely the slave catcher would not be able to talk the Federal marshal into coming out in this. Would the Stearnses' friends with the boat come? And if not, what should we do next?

The storm was on us quickly, and just as quickly, the slave catcher was banging at the door. I stood in the parlor, looking out the window. As lightning lit the sky, I could see the outline of the big elm tree, which stands leaning on the very bank of the canal. Even knowing where to look, I could not make out the shadows that were Adah and Marella.

I turned my back to the window and pretended to warm my hands at the fireplace as the two men who were hunting Adah entered the room. In truth, I was so afraid I felt nothing.

"Nasty night," said the slave catcher, trying to be civil now that he had gotten his way.

Rebekka clung in fear to my skirts as the men looked behind drapes and chairs. Jacob we had sent up-stairs and to bed, telling him he was to answer any questions by saying, "I am not allowed to speak after my bedtime."

Theodore delayed the men as much as possible, talking all the while and demanding that they look in every impossible corner and underneath every little table so that should they decide to search the grounds beyond the barn, which they had searched before ever coming inside, Adah and her child might be safely away by then or, at least, their footprints washed away by the rain. The three men clattered through the downstairs, the upstairs, and the attic before I saw the flicker of light by the elm. There was a particularly bright flash of lightning, almost simultaneous with an explosive clap of thunder. Hurry, hurry, I urged her in my mind, pretending to be rearranging the table lamp as the men came downstairs and headed down to the cellar.

And then there was another flash of lightning, except that this time it did not harmlessly light up the sky. It struck the elm tree. Even from this far away I could hear, after the thunder, the crack of the wood itself, the tree splitting. I had shut my eyes against the bright flash, but though I reopened them immediately I could not find the spot of light that was Adah's lantern.

"Stay here," I commanded Rebekka. I ran outside, all the while trying to convince myself that, after traveling for so long and through such difficulty to reach safety, Adah had simply dropped the lantern in startlement. Outside the wind tugged at my hair and clothing, the rain pelted my face, and the mud sucked at my shoes.

At the canal's edge, the elm had been cut in half. That part that normally faced the canal was hanging in the water, still attached to the trunk by thick wooden threads. The remainder of the tree was tipped almost entirely over, its roots up in the air, glistening with mud. A whole section of the canal bank was gone, having slid into the water.

From the water, from the canal boat sent to rescue Adah and Marella, someone was clanging a bell. A voice called out to me, "They're in the water. Can you see them?"

I stepped too close to the edge, and felt the mud shifting under my foot. I grabbed hold of the tree and felt it give under my weight, but then it caught and held fast. "Adah!" I cried out. "Marella!"

"My God," someone on the boat called to me, a second man, I thought, though I could not see, "I think they're under all that mud."

They could not be, I thought. Surely they could not be. The tree gave another loud crack. I backed away, though that took me even further from helping them. If I looked hard enough, I thought, I would find them. It was simply a matter of looking and I have always been good at finding lost things. "Adah!" I called. Why did they not answer?

With one final crack, the broken part of the tree snapped off and slid down the steep bank the rest of the way into the water. But it happened too late to be of any good to the remainder of the tree. "Stand back!" one of the men yelled out. "Stand back! Stand back!" And with that, the tree tipped the rest of the way over and crashed into the water, taking another section of the bank with it. "No!" I screamed. How could I ever find Adah and Marella if things kept falling into the water?

"Someone is coming," one of the men in the boat said. "Friend, is that your husband?"

I could hear the boatman, I could understand what he was saying, I could tell that he wanted to be reassured it wasn't slave catchers approaching, but I couldn't answer, I couldn't stop crying.

It was only when I heard the oars hitting the water and I realized they were leaving that I was able to catch my breath, that I was able to call after them, "Don't go, you can't just leave them."

They did not answer, they did not come back, and in a moment I felt Theodore's arms around me. "The slave catchers are gone," he said. "What happened?"

"They're in the water," I said, beating away his hands because he was holding me back. "I need to get closer so I can find them. They'll come up for air any moment now. They have to. We know their names. I'll find them if I look hard enough."

After a while Theodore picked me up and carried me back into the house.

CHAPTER 14

Jackie Comes to the Rescue (Sort Of)

I FOUND I COULDN'T sit still.

I put the journal down and started pacing back and forth, to work off some of my nervous energy, before I realized I probably shouldn't leave the book untended, since the ghost—Adah; now I knew her name—since Adah had seemed so intent on preventing me from getting it in the first place. Not that there was anything in what I had just read that gave any indication Adah would harm the book. I snatched the journal up, anyway, and held it close. There was nothing in what I had just read that gave any indication that Adah would do any of the things she had been doing for the last several days.

"What's going on?" I asked out loud, just in case Adah decided to explain all.

She didn't.

I pictured her as Winifred had first described her:

standing in the cold, having given up her blanket for Marella to have two. I remembered how she had refused to say anything against her Southern master. Either she'd totally fooled Winifred, or maybe dying had changed her. Never having died myself, I was willing to grant that dying might have a bad effect on someone's personality.

It was already a quarter past two. Vicki would be home in another half hour, and Zach shortly after that, unless he had detention again. It's hard to keep up with Zach's detentions. Regardless of what Winifred thought, Adah was getting more and more dangerous, and I couldn't just sit around waiting to see what she would do next and who she'd do it to.

Jackie, I thought. Jackie would have ideas.

Jackie lives just close enough to her school that she gets to ride a bus, but she's the last one on in the morning and the first one off in the afternoon. Still, when I called her number, she wasn't home yet and the answering machine kicked in. It's in Jackie's room, and I hoped it would be Jackie who played back the message, because if it was Aunt Rose or Uncle Bob, boy would I feel like an idiot.

Not having any idea how long a message the machine was set to take, I talked fast. "Jac, this is very important. I found Great-Great-Grandmother Winifred's diary, which tells all about how the ghosts came to be ghosts. But it's getting really spooky around here. Adah—that's the mother ghost—she tried to drown me in my dreams, except that it really made me sick, which shows she's getting stronger or something. First she was able to flip a board, and now she can move keys, and she threw some boxes at me. My parents are next to useless because they don't believe anything I say about this, and the journal won't help, because it just says what a nice person Adah was. And I don't know what to do." I was running out of words. "Do you have any ideas?" I asked lamely. "Call me back, will you?"

I set the phone down and looked at the journal some more.

By two-forty, all that I'd learned was that Winifred felt that she and her family had made things worse than they were and she was determined never to get involved with smuggling runaways again. There was absolutely nothing to indicate that at that time Adah and Marella were still...hanging around. Between the fallen tree and all the mud from the collapsing canal bank, not to mention that Winifred and Theodore didn't dare make too big a deal of looking for bodies because it would prove they were helping runaways, which was illegal, it didn't sound as if the bodies were ever found.

Maybe that was it. Maybe the ghosts weren't at rest because their bodies had never been buried.

But then, why did they choose *now* to start haunting?

People from the canal authority had called the tree a hazard to navigation and they'd hauled the tree out before Winifred had resumed writing in her diary; but maybe it had taken this long for the weather to wear away the mud. Maybe the bones had been covered then, but now they weren't.

But if that was it, why had the ghosts briefly appeared to Jackie eight years ago, only to disappear, only to reappear?

The more I thought, the more confused I got, and then Vicki came home. Just as I was letting her in, the phone rang.

Jackie! I thought, lunging for the phone. But it was only Dad, calling to see how I was—and putting off his next repair order, which was for a woman who claimed she had no phone but kept hearing a phone ringing. After assuring Dad that I was fine, I was just handing Vicki the phone when the doorbell rang, and there was Jackie.

"*Jaclyn,*" Jackie said as soon as I opened the front door. "The name is Jaclyn. I know it's hard for someone of your limited intelligence to grasp words with more than one syllable, but try it slowly: Jaaac-lynnnn."

Beyond her I could see Aunt Rose, sitting in their car waiting for the traffic to clear enough to pull out of the driveway. Seeing me, she beeped and waved.

"Are you going to let us in?" Jackie asked, still on the other side of the screen door. "Or is your little brain still trying to process my name?"

" 'Us'?" I repeated, a second before a dog barked and I realized that Jackie hadn't developed sudden curvature of the spine but was leaned over, holding on to Cinnamon's collar.

Jackie sighed, opened the door herself, and came in, dragging along Cinnamon, who was busy sniffing the welcome mat as though it was the most fascinating thing she'd smelled all day.

Knowing how Jackie felt about our house, I was so relieved to see her that I threw my arms around her before even giving her a chance to disentangle herself from her backpack.

"Back off." She planted her hand on my chest and pushed me away. She was dressed, as usual, like a mourner at her own funeral. Her fingernails were painted chrome.

"Thank you," I said. "For coming."

"Yeah, well," Jackie said, fidgeting with her jacket.

By then Vicki was through on the phone. "Cinnamon!" she squealed, ignoring Jackie as though Cinnamon had walked here on her own. "Can I take Cinnamon outside, Jackie?"

Jackie shook her head. "No, Cinnamon doesn't know enough to stay out of a busy street."

"Why'd you bring her?" I asked.

"Animals can sense things people can't," Jackie said, giving me a long, meaningful stare. "They act strange around otherworldly beings." *Ghosts,* I guessed she was saying. But Cinnamon's one of those big dumb dogs that's always twitching and drooling and chasing her own tail. How could we ever guess if she was acting stranger than that?

"Can I go out and play?" Vicki asked.

"No," I said, thinking I wanted her closer by than that.

"Just on the swing set."

That was halfway to the canal ditch. "No," I said.

"I'm going to tell Daddy."

"Don't you dare bother him at work two minutes after he just called us."

"Teddy, you're so mean. I'm going to tell Daddy when he gets home." Vicki stomped up the stairs. "Or Mommy," she added, and slammed the door to her room.

Cinnamon, in the meantime, had jumped up onto the couch, which would have made my mother crazy if she'd been there to see. Jackie pulled Winifred's journal out from underneath my arm and plunked herself down next to Cinnamon, which left no room for me.

"July third," I told her. I leaned over the back of the couch. She seemed to have a lot less trouble than I did making out the handwriting. "There was a part earlier," I said, "where the neighbor woman, Naomi Stearns, asked them to take in a runaway slave woman and her child because the Stearnses' house was being watched by slave catchers. Apparently the Stearnses' did this on a regular basis."

Jackie nodded without looking up.

"I guess there was some sort of law that said people couldn't help slaves."

"Fugitive Slave Act of 1850," Jackie said, still not looking up.

Big deal. She's in eighth grade. She's supposed to know stuff like that. I'm supposed to know Luxembourg.

When Jackie was near the section where Winifred asked their names, I explained, "There was another part where they helped a black man who just showed up in their barn. They helped him escape, but Winifred felt bad that she'd never gotten around to asking his name."

Jackie ignored me.

A page later, I said, "*Mulatto* means half white and half black."

"I know what it means," Jackie snapped impatiently.

So I didn't say anything else. I just stood behind her, biting at a piece of skin near my thumbnail until she was finished.

"I've made it to the end of July," I said as she flipped through the next few pages, "and there isn't anything about strange dreams or visions, or unexplainable things going on."

"She mention the kids?"

"Just that they were upset."

Jackie didn't take my word for it but skimmed the whole rest of the book. She never acknowledged that I was right but, in the end, just set the book down and said, "So tell me exactly what happened that got you so"—she wiggled her chrome fingertips—"hyper."

I told her all about it: the dream where I'd sucked in the water that Marella had drowned in—before I ever knew that Marella had drowned in real life—and how I'd choked on it and thrown up ("Gee, Ted," Jackie said, "thank you for sharing that"), and how I'd learned about the journal from Grandma and Granddad, and what had happened in the attic.

"But she didn't do anything once you actually got the book?" Jackie asked.

"No," I admitted. "What do you think it all means?"

"I think it means we have a crazy ghost on our hands," Jackie said. "That's why Marella is afraid of her."

"You mean dying made Adah crazy?"

"Or being not-quite-dead all these years."

"Not-quite-dead sounds suspiciously like vampires," I said. I found my hand straying to my neck.

Jackie sighed loudly. "Forget the vampires. Look, when you die, you're supposed to kind of...move on...to heaven, right?"

"Or not," I pointed out.

Jackie gave me a dirty look. "Anyway, obviously Adah and Marella didn't move on anywhere. Maybe because they died violently or because they were never properly buried. Whatever the reason, the two of them are obviously stuck somewhere between being alive and being dead. Just the two of them, because, obviously, one of the rules of being a ghost must be you have to stay near where you died. Obviously, Adah and Marella are both lonely. But the difference is, every time there's a little girl about her age in this house, Marella tries to contact her to play with her."

"Ahhh," I said, suddenly getting it.

"But, obviously,"—Jackie could use the word *obviously* about things that weren't at all obvious more often than anybody else in the world—"the mother is jealous and doesn't want Marella talking to anybody but her."

"Because," I said, and Jackie joined in so we both finished together, "she's crazy."

It fit better than any theory *I* had. "So what do we do?"

"Obviously, an exorcism."

"Call in a priest?" I asked. Somehow I couldn't picture myself picking up the phone and inviting over Father D., our sixty-year-old pastor. "Oh, and by the way," I'd have to tell him, "don't mention this to my parents."

But Jackie was shaking her head. "Oh, Ted," she said, "you always make everything so complicated. One of us came prepared." She got off the couch, which woke up Cinnamon, who began bounding around the family room while Jackie fetched her backpack. Jackie held up a tiny bottle.

"Perfume?" I guessed.

Obviously not. "Souvenir holy water," she said with a sigh. "Don't you remember when Aunt Len went with that church group to Lourdes?"

I didn't bother to point out that Len is her mother's sister and therefore no relation to me at all; and, no, I did not remember when she went to Lourdes.

Cinnamon was so eager to see what Jackie was doing, she tried to stick her head in the backpack, and Jackie had to push her away.

"Ghost-repelling music," Jackie said, pulling out a cassette tape.

"What's ghost-repelling music?" I asked. "Do you mean religious songs?"

"Opera," she said.

"How about Christmas carols?" I said. "We've got John Denver and the Muppets singing 'Silent Night.' Maybe that'd do better?"

"Opera," Jackie repeated, forcing me to take her tape. "Opera will drive *anybody* out of the house. Don't put it on till the last minute."

The next thing she pulled out was a mirror, the small round kind with a handle. The next thing after that was another mirror, one with a little metal stand. After that, she pulled out yet another mirror, this one set in the middle of a stained-glass daisy pattern, which I recognized to be the one that normally hung on her bedroom wall. She also had two tiny mirrors in cases, the kind girls carry in their purses. Jackie set the mirrors faceup in a semicircle around her. "We need to complete the circle with more mirrors," she said.

"How come?"

"To form a barrier around us, which the ghosts can't cross."

"This is getting to sound like vampires again," I muttered.

"Just get some," she said. She picked up the backpack and dumped the rest of the contents onto the floor. Candles. Lots and lots of candles. Ever since the ice storm that left the entire city of Rochester without electricity for a week, everyone always has candles.

I got the mirror from the vanity brush-and-comb set Zach and I bought Mom for Christmas last year, and the mirror from by the front door in the living room, which has a sunset painted on it. That wasn't enough to close the circle—and meanwhile Jackie had gotten dishes from the kitchen cupboard and was busy setting lit candles on them, making an outer circle beyond the one with the mirrors, which made me nervous with Cinnamon sniffing and poking around—so I hurriedly pulled the entire medicine cabinet Zach had made in shop off its hook in the powder room.

"There," I said.

"Good," Jackie said. Apparently it was the first thing I'd done right. "Now put on the tape."

Mercifully, the stereo was in the living room. But Jackie called, "Louder." And, "Louder." And again,

"LOUDER." Till I could feel the bass rumbling in my bones.

Back in the family room, Jackie had opened all the windows and the sliding glass door.

"Jeez," I said, hugging myself for warmth and shouting to be heard over Luciano Pavarotti, "it's only March, you know. It's forty degrees out there." Dad hadn't even put in the screens yet.

"We have to leave an exit route for the ghosts. Cinnamon, get away from there."

I grabbed Cinnamon by the collar before she could make it outside, and slid the door till it was open only a couple inches. I didn't use the screen panel because Cinnamon is just dumb enough that I was afraid she'd jump through it. "Here," I said, knowing we had to make a diversion for Cinnamon and knowing that she had a thing for socks. I pulled off my sock, tied a knot in it, and tossed it into the kitchen.

She went skittering after it, her nails clicking on the floor.

Jackie put the back of her hand to her forehead, like one of those old-time actresses in a black-and-white movie. "That's disgusting," she said.

"Yeah, well, let's get going before she comes back."

"Come into the circle," Jackie said, "and sit back-to-back with me."

But just as I was shifting balance to step over the double circle of candles and mirrors, she said, "Bible."

" 'Bible' ?" I repeated.

"One of us will sit on the journal," she said, indicating it on the floor next to her, "the other on the Bible. That way, we and the journal will all be safe. You *do* have a Bible, don't you?"

"Sure." I considered. "Somewhere."

Jackie sighed. "Never mind, then."

"No, hold on." I ran to the kitchen desk, where the mail, and grocery-store coupons, and all sorts of papers accumulate. I brought back a stack of church bulletins. "Is this close enough?" I asked.

Jackie sighed, but she took them to sit on, because they were less lumpy than the journal.

As soon as I sat down, she stood up, holding the bottle from Lourdes. She reached over the mirrors and the candles, then dribbled the liquid out in a third circle.

Holy water better not leave a stain, I thought, *or Mom's going to kill you.*

Jackie sat down again and reached behind, for my hands. "Close your eyes and concentrate," she said, but she didn't say what to concentrate on.

"Aren't we supposed to be sitting around a table?" I asked. "So that the ghosts can bang out messages on the wood?"

"Don't be more of an idiot than is absolutely necessary, Ted. This is an exorcism, not a seance." Then she called out in a loud voice, "Oh, spirits that haunt this house, we call you by name, Adah and Marella, and we say unto you, get thee hence."

" 'Hence'?" I said.

Jackie dug her fingernails into my hand.

I squirmed but she wouldn't let me go.

"And again, we say it unto you," she repeated, shouting for dramatic effect, I guess, or maybe just to drown out Pavarotti, "Adah and Marella, get thee hence. Three times we name you, Adah and Marella, and three times we command you, GET...THEE...HENCE!"

By chance or design, her last words coincided with the last notes of the aria that was currently playing on the tape. Good timing. Because if it hadn't been for that moment of silence, we never would have heard the sound of banging.

CHAPTER 15

Our TV Tunes in a Channel Nobody Else's TV Gets

THE NEXT BIT OF operatic dish-rattling began, but by then we were listening for it: a definite knocking on wood. I tightened my grip on Jackie's suddenly sweaty hand. The sound seemed to be coming from the living room and, for the moment at least, it didn't seem to be moving closer to us in the family room.

"Now what?" I asked, my throat so dry I was surprised I was able to get the words out.

I could feel that Jackie was shaking, but she kept her voice steady. "That depends on what she's saying."

"She's angry," I said, which was obvious enough from the loudness and speed at which the banging occurred, and the fact that it kept on and on.

"What else?" she asked.

"What do you mean, 'What else'? How am I supposed to know?"

"Isn't it Morse code?" she asked as though that were the next logical question.

"I don't know," I stammered. "I don't know Morse code."

"Oh, well, that's great," she said, like it was all my fault. "I thought all boys knew Morse code—dot-dot-dash and all that nonsense."

"That's the most ridiculous thing I've ever heard," I said. "And even if I knew Morse code, what makes you think ghosts automatically know it, too? And, besides, this doesn't sound like Morse code; it just sounds like a lot of angry banging."

"Well, now we'll never know, will we?" Then, as I tried to pull my hand out of hers, she hurriedly said, "Don't let go. You'll break the protection spell."

"I take it back," I said. "*That's* the most ridiculous thing I've ever heard." But I didn't pull away. "Maybe she's angry about the music. That would explain why she's in there and hasn't come in here. If she knocks down the shelf with the tape player, my dad is going to go through the roof."

"Ted," Jackie said, "from the sound of her, if she wanted to knock down the tape player, it'd be down by now."

True. "So what do *you* think she's doing?"

"Maybe she's banging on the walls, trying to get out," Jackie said. "Maybe she doesn't know we've got the door and windows open in here."

"She's never had trouble going through walls before," I pointed out.

Jackie ignored me. "Once the tape ends, maybe she'll come in here."

"How long's the tape?"

"Sixty minutes," Jackie said.

"Forget it." Our hands were so slick with sweat, I slipped loose of her grip. "By then we'll either be dead of fear or totally deaf."

"Ted, don't break the circle!" she cried, trying to keep me from standing. "I don't have any more holy water."

"Then you stay in here." I tucked the journal in my belt and stepped over the ring of mirrors, and then over the ring of candles. My one sockless foot landed right in the ring of holy water.

Jackie sighed. "Once the circle's broken, it's useless."

All in all, she must have decided it'd be best to know what was coming, for she followed me to the living room.

I took one hesitant step in, but two real quick ones back, which of course landed me on Jackie's feet. But she'd seen it, too, I could tell, and she moved back without complaining or making snide remarks. There was a big black shadow, human-sized and vaguely human-shaped, hovering on the frosted glass of the front door.

"She's trying to get in, not out," Jackie hissed at me. "And you broke the circle!" She pinched my arm.

But that wasn't it. Now that we were in the living room, with Luciano Pavarotti battering our eardrums and the banging turning our knees to Jell-O, I could hear something else.

I could hear Zach shouting from the wrong side of the door, "Ted, you stupid little toad! Once I get inside, I'm going to flush you down the toilet!"

Which was probably not the most convincing argument he could have used to get me to let him in.

Still, I couldn't see that delaying would do anything to improve the situation.

"It's Zach," I said, shoving Jackie in front of me. "You let him in. He's less likely to hit you."

To my amazement, she actually did what I told her. Not that it helped. As soon as she'd unlocked the door, Zach gave a great shove, which flung the door entirely open and pinned Jackie behind it smack up against the closet door.

Which left me facing Zach, alone.

"You little..." he started. But it wasn't brotherly compassion that stopped him. "*What*," he demanded, "are you listening to?"

From behind the door, Jackie said, "*Luciano Pavarotti—Live on Stage.*"

Zach pulled the door back so he could see her. "You're both crazy," he said. "You've got bad taste *and* you're crazy. And you're going to blow the speakers." He hit the stereo's eject button, cutting Pavarotti off midsyllable. "What could you possibly have been think-ing of?"

"Ghost-repelling music," I said.

"*What?*"

"Ghost-repelling music," I repeated. "Tell him, Jackie."

Jackie just shrugged, as though it had all been my idea.

So I went on without her. "Listen, Zach—"

"I don't want to hear it."

I pulled Winifred's journal out from under my belt and waved it in Zach's face.

He took a step back and smacked my hand away from him. "Ah, that stinks. What is that?"

"Great-Great-Grandmother Winifred's diary," I said. "And it proves that Vicki and I haven't been making things up. Winifred was helping runaway slaves, and one of them was a little girl named Marella who died in the canal just behind our house. And her mother died there, too."

"I didn't even know we had a great-great-grandmother Winifred," Zach said.

Leave it to Zach to pick up the one least important thing that I'd said. "Wake-up call for Zach Beatson," I said, waving the book under his nose again. "Don't you think it's a coincidence that Vicki chose for her so-called imaginary friend the same name as that of another five-year-old who just happened to die here almost a hun-dred fifty years ago?"

"Maybe she read the book and that's where she got the name."

"Zach, she's five years old. She can just barely read her own name."

Zach moved to get by me, but I blocked his way. "There's a point to all this, I imagine?" he said. "Would you get that thing away from me? It smells like something's burning or something."

Jackie and I looked at each other, because the book only smelled like dust, not smoke.

"The candles," Jackie gasped.

"Cinnamon," I gasped.

We ran into the family room, but there was no sign of Jackie's dog, and all of the candles were still upright on their plates, except that one had just sputtered out and was smoking, which was what we had smelled.

"Oh boy," Zach said with glee. "Mom and Dad are going to kill you when they see this."

"We were doing an exorcism," I told him.

He flung himself on the couch and reached for the remote control. "Well, you should have done it at Jackie's house," he said.

Jackie began blowing out the candles.

"Would you just look at the book?" I begged.

"I'd rather look at *Jerry Springer*," he said. "Today it's 'Sisterhood of Crime: When Nuns Go Bad.'" He clicked the channel button. "What did you do to the TV? Did you exorcise that, too?"

The screen was all staticky, the way it looks when you put in a blank videotape.

"We didn't do anything," I protested.

He clicked the VCR button on, then off again.

Jackie looked up from blowing out candles. "I think I can make something out, real fuzzy, right in the center," she said.

"Oxygen deprivation," Zach said. But I thought I could see it, too, and he must have also because he fiddled with some more of the buttons. The sound hissed and crackled; the black-and-white static danced all over the screen.

"Maybe the cable's out," I suggested.

Zach switched to the regular stations and flipped through them. Still a lot of static, but now there was definitely something in the middle. Zach went back to cable. "I'd swear it looks like a person," he said.

My thought exactly. My stomach was beginning to feel all funny again, for the first time since last night.

Zach was saying, "But why the same thing on all channels? Unless it's the president announcing we're at war or something."

"Zach, turn it off," I said.

"Maybe the Ginna Nuclear Power Plant exploded," Zach continued as though I wasn't there. "And by tonight we'll all glow in the dark."

"Zach, turn off the TV."

"What's that channel they're always saying to turn to if there's a national disaster?"

"ZACH, TURN OFF THE TV!" I screamed at him.

That finally got his attention, but he just turned and looked at me like he couldn't believe I'd talk to him that way.

Over his shoulder I could see the person on the TV coming in clearer every second, walking toward us through the field of static, a dark silhouette in a long gown and bonnet.

Jackie took the remote control out of Zach's hand and turned off the power.

Zach opened his mouth to protest but didn't say a word. The screen stayed the same: black-and-white static with someone coming straight toward us.

With Marella's mother coming straight toward us.

Closer.

Closer.

Till her face filled the screen.

Till, with a flash of white smoke and silver sparks, her image burst out of the TV and into the family room.

We didn't even have a chance to duck. She swooped through me, a clammy tingle that left the taste of murky water in my mouth; then, before I had the chance to do anything—pass out was what I assumed I'd do as soon as I had a second—she swept through Zach, then Jackie, then stood there shimmering and hazy in the middle of the room, hovering an inch or two above the floor.

All things considered, she didn't look as frightening as I had anticipated. I mean, sure, I was scared stiff, but she looked more sad than angry. Even her clothes, her long black dress and her bonnet, looked tired, hanging limply as though—I thought stupidly for a second—she'd been caught in the rain. And then I remembered what she had been caught in. I saw water dripping from the hem of the ruffle Winifred had added to her dress, dripping and never reaching the rug beneath.

Her voice came thin and scratchy, as if from an antique recording. "Canal," she said.

We all leaned closer. "What?" I asked, amazing myself that my own voice worked, amazing myself that I could even breathe.

"Canal," she repeated, becoming more see-through as though the effort of speaking cost too much energy. "Stop. *Stop*. CANAL."

The others didn't look like they were capable of saying anything. I managed to squeak, "I don't understand."

And then she did look angry.

She swept at me again, and I lost sight of her.

I whirled around, but she wasn't there. I figured I was too scared to see straight. But then I felt her tugging and clawing inside my brain. She hadn't come out the other side. I was being smothered. "No," I managed to gasp. Blackness crowded the edges of my vision, closing in, closing in, until all I could see was darkness, except for one small area of brightness like light reflected off dark water. I concentrated on that brightness, figuring if I lost consciousness, that'd be the end of me. I looked at the light, and looked at the light, and it became white bones, gleaming on the hillside.

"Stop it!" I'm not sure if I shouted it out loud or only said it in my mind. "Go away!"

And she did.

Once again she hovered in the middle of the room, but so faintly I could barely see her. She reached out to me. Her lips formed what may well have been the word *canal*, and then she faded away entirely.

I didn't pass out, after all.

If I looked half as bad as Zach and Jackie, I'm surprised they didn't pass out at the sight of me.

I wrapped my arms around myself, though the cold came from inside me, not outside. I remembered that Jackie had opened the back door and the windows, and it was good to have something—somebody—to blame the cold on. But the sliding glass door was completely closed, which none of the three of us had done. And then, finally, I noticed that, for at least the last couple minutes, I'd been hearing a dog barking outside.

At which point I looked out the door and saw that Cinnamon was standing at the edge of the canal ditch, barking like crazy.

I was too far away to see if her fur was standing on end, but my hair sure was.

Cinnamon backed up, backed up, but never stopped barking.

A hand grasped the branch of one of the bushes that grew at the edge of the ditch. The top of someone's head appeared—someone climbing up out of the ditch. I thought that it'd be nice to be able to pass out at will.

"Vicki," Zach said in a voice little more than a sigh.

I heard Jackie release a breath and realized I'd been holding mine, too. Now I let it go. Vicki, and not Adah, and not a collection of walking bones bleached white by the sun. Vicki had sneaked out despite my telling her not to—it had to have been while we were in the living room letting Zach in—and she had nearly made me die of a heart attack. As I watched her walk slowly toward the house, I couldn't make up my mind if I wanted to hug her or strangle her.

Vicki must have seen us watching, she must be intentionally walking slowly to delay her punishment, for she just strolled, looking from side to side as though she'd never seen our yard before.

I forced my mind to stay with that thought—Vicki was trying to delay her punishment—and wouldn't let myself think of anything else, wouldn't wonder what she'd been doing down in that ditch where we'd never let her go by herself before, when she'd never shown any interest in the old canal before.

And I definitely wouldn't let myself wonder where Adah had gotten to or why Cinnamon wouldn't get near Vicki and yet wouldn't stop barking.

And then Vicki was at the door. Her shoes were all muddy, her hands were muddy—she even had mud splattered on her face. There was no way she could proclaim to be innocent. She put one muddy hand out and touched the glass, as though a glass door was the most wonderful thing she'd ever seen. But then she got distracted and just stared at her hand. Finally, she cocked her head and looked at me, as though studying my face for an upcoming exam.

I slid the door open, and she just looked at me for several more long seconds before she stepped in.

By then the hair on my arms once again felt as though it was standing at attention.

Very slowly, very calmly, she said, "Hello, Theodore."

CHAPTER 16

Jackie and I Visit the Canal

FIVE OR SIX SECONDS passed before I could get my voice working. What I said, when I finally said it, was, "Hello, Adah."

Vicki smiled, a quirky smile unlike any expression I'd ever seen on Vicki's face before. "Don't be silly," she said in a voice which was perfectly hers, even though the tone wasn't. "Adah's dead." She glanced at each of the others. "Hello, Zachary. Hello, Jaclyn."

Zach and Jackie didn't do any better than I had. They just sat there on the couch with their mouths open.

Vicki gave a polite nod, another gesture totally unlike her, and walked through the family room and up the stairs. She wouldn't have fooled us for a minute, even if we hadn't seen what we'd just seen. When she got to her room, she closed her door behind her.

Zach finally managed to close his mouth. "What," he said, his voice quavering, "is going on?"

"If you stop and think about it," Jackie snapped, all bristly now that the crisis had peaked, "I think you can pretty well see what's going on. The thing we have to figure out is how to stop it."

"Yeah?" Zach said, obviously stung by her tone but unable to come up with a suitably cutting reply. "Yeah?"

I jumped in before they could get sidetracked with taking shots at each other. "What I think Zach is trying to say is, How are we going to stop it?"

Despite the fact that Jackie was sitting and I was standing, I had the distinct impression she looked down her nose at me. "Obviously," she said, "we need another exorcism. The circle will be stronger with three of us in it. In the meantime, I'll relight the candles. Zach, you need to stand guard by Vicki's door to make sure she doesn't try to escape. Ted, you can bike over to the church and steal some holy water from those little containers by the doors."

"We're going to sprinkle Vicki with holy water?" Zach asked.

"No," Jackie and I answered together.

"It's part of the magic circle," Jackie explained, "to make sure Adah's ghost doesn't come out of Vicki and into one of us."

"No," I said again. "Jackie, the exorcism couldn't have had anything to do with it. We saw Adah after the exorcism was over."

"Yeah," Jackie said, "and the instant Adah disappeared, Vicki popped out of the ditch."

"But she'd already gone down there on her own. And come most of the way back up."

"I can't understand any of this," Zach said.

"Neither can I," I admitted. "And Jackie's only bluffing her way through."

Jackie gave her shocked-and-amazed-that-anybody-could-say-such-a-thing look, but she didn't deny it.

"So what's the next step?" Zach asked. "Am I supposed to get the holy water, or what?"

"*Ted*," Jackie corrected him. "Ted is supposed to get the holy water. *You're* supposed to guard Vicki's door."

"I knew that," Zach said. He started up the stairs.

Meanwhile, I was working real hard at trying to ignore the gnawing suspicion that I knew what the next step might be, and that it wasn't what Jackie thought it was. But I couldn't ignore the memory of what it had felt like to have Adah working at my mind, trying to claw her way in. Was Vicki still inside her own head somewhere, pushed aside and held down, frightened and thinking she was alone and maybe wondering if any of us could even tell that it wasn't her looking out through those eyes of hers or if she would be kept prisoner where she was forever?

I blurted it out. "Whatever happened to Vicki, it happened down by the old canal."

Zach and Jackie just looked at me.

I thought of Adah trying to claw into my head and how I never wanted to feel anything like that again. But then there was Vicki.

I said, "I think I need to go down there."

The two of them exchanged a worried look.

Jackie sighed. She gulped. She momentarily shut her eyes. "All right," she said.

"Does that mean I get the holy water and you guard her door?" Zach asked Jackie. "Or does that mean you get the holy water and I guard the door?"

"Nobody's getting holy water," Jackie said. "We're going with Ted."

"No," I said. I knew it was ridiculous for all of us to walk into that danger, but it would have been nice to have to argue with them a bit. "You go ahead and guard her door, Zach. We can't lose track of her now. Jackie... you do whatever you think needs to be done."

"I'll come with you," she whispered.

It was such a welcome relief, I hesitated, and she added, getting steadier with each word, "Yeah, yeah, I know. But if we sent you down there by yourself and you tripped over your shoelace and broke your neck, how would we ever know?"

"Uhm, well, thanks," I said.

"Guard the door?" Zach said, sounding guilty and relieved and guilty-to-be-relieved all at the same time. "You're sure?"

"Guard the door," Jackie and I echoed.

Zach nodded and planted himself in front of Vicki's door, his arms crossed in front of his chest like Mr. Clean.

Whatever happened now, I'd asked for it.

I got my sneakers from the mudroom, off the kitchen. The sock Cinnamon had been playing with was all slobbery, so I ended up putting my sneakers on with one socked foot and one bare foot. I told myself there was no time to go upstairs for a fresh sock, but the truth of it was I didn't want to walk past Vicki's room. Much as I dreaded going down to the canal, I had to admit to myself that I wouldn't have wanted Zach's job, either.

Outside, the air was chilly, though the sun made it seem warmer than it really was. The trees were still bare from winter, the grass all flattened out and brownish from the snow that had melted away only last week.

Cinnamon, who'd plunked herself down several feet away from the house, got up and approached warily. We held our hands out for her to sniff. Reassured that it was really us, she gave one halfhearted bark and slowly wagged her tail.

But she stopped wagging and stopped following when she saw that we were headed for the edge of the ditch. She sat down and began that low mournful moaning dogs sometimes do: the sound that—after about ten seconds—makes you want to throw a bucket of cold water at them.

There was a good spot for getting down into the ditch, right on the border between our yard and the Wienckis', a trail formed and kept clear of vegetation by butts sliding down and feet climbing up, through two generations of Beatsons and one of Wienckis.

Jackie, who wasn't used to it, clung to branches and

dug her sneakered feet into the dirt and generally looked like she was mentally kicking herself for agreeing to come.

The whole bottom of the ditch was filled with muddy, murky water—about two feet deep in the middle and stretching across at least twenty to twenty-five feet. In the winter you can ice-skate on it, but by summer the water would be gone. Everything looked pretty much as it always does in earliest spring: scrubby little bushes that you'd swear must be dead but always come back, lots of rocks and dead leaves, and mud everywhere. At the moment, there were some beer cans half submerged in the water at the far edge, which had to be from the slobs in the development behind us. The Wiencki kids are getting too old to come down here anymore, and Zach and I have too much class to litter. Or to drink beer.

It was easy to follow Vicki's footprints in the mud. Almost to the water, she had veered off the path and headed in the direction that led directly behind our house. With the mud trying to suck my shoes off my feet, I followed, with Jackie huffing and puffing right behind me.

We were headed toward something on the bank. At first I figured Vicki had brought down some sort of snack, sat down in the mud to eat, and then left the box or bag down here. Vicki is enough of a slob that it made sense.

But as we got closer, I saw that wasn't it at all. Vicki

had been digging in the side of the bank, which explained her muddy hands, and what she'd uncovered were bones, which may have explained a lot more.

I stopped, unable to bring myself to go any closer. They were all brown and brittle looking. No skulls showed, but that didn't matter. I knew they were human, and I knew whose they had to be.

Behind me, Jackie asked, "Do you think if we rebury them, she'll go away?"

"No." I told her. "I've been down here a million times, ever since I was five or six. I *know* these bones haven't been lying here out in the open since the time you first saw the ghosts. They weren't here this past fall."

"Yeah, but maybe it's because they're out in the open that Adah had the strength to take over Vicki's body."

I rubbed my hands over my face, trying to concentrate. "But if Adah wasn't in Vicki until Vicki uncovered the bones,"—I turned back to look at Jackie—"then why did Vicki uncover the bones?"

Jackie started to shake her head. Then I saw her eyes move to focus on a spot over my left shoulder. Her eyes got real big and I knew what to expect even before I turned.

It was Adah, hovering palely over the bones.

I took a hasty step back, ready to run, but she made no move to follow.

Which was good, because I don't really think my wobbly legs would have carried me far.

She reached out to me, then brought her hands back to touch at where her heart would be if she'd had one. She indicated the bones, then brought her hands up to her face.

"Watch out," Jackie said. "She's putting some sort of spell on us."

"No, she's not," I said. When she touched her cheeks, it drew my attention to the fact that she didn't look angry and fierce. She looked sad and—hard as it was to believe—frightened. Surely not of us. But then, what? I said, "She's trying to tell us something."

Adah nodded.

"What?" I asked her. Was I up to facing what could frighten a ghost?

She crouched down and touched the bones, her hand passing right through them. Again her hand went to her breast, then she held her hand parallel with the ground but up higher than her shoulder. She pointed at the water. Then, once again, she gestured toward the bones.

"They're your bones," I said.

She nodded.

"Yours and Marella's"—I felt incredibly strange saying it—"after...after you drowned."

Once more she nodded. And once more she touched the bones. This time she pointed to me before holding her hand up in the same little-child gesture she had done before. And now she pointed up the hill, in the direction of our house.

"Vicki?" I said. "You're saying something about Vicki, but I don't understand the rest."

Adah touched the bones with both hands.

"Vicki touched the bones?" I asked.

Nodding, Adah indicated herself, then gave the sign for little child and pointed toward the house.

I took in a deep breath. "Marella."

Adah nodded.

Jackie had crowded up behind me and now she said, "You mean it's Marella who's taken Vicki's body?"

Adah nodded.

"Ted," Jackie said, "what if she's lying?"

"If she's lying, then who *is* in Vicki's body, with Adah down here with us?"

Adah was still crouched by the bones. Instead of floating, her feet—and, in fact, the lower part of her body—seemed to be half swallowed up by the mud.

It must be hard to stay level, I thought, when you can't feel the ground.

It must be hard to communicate when you can't talk and when people scream and carry on every time you try.

Suddenly everything fell into place. "You were trying to warn us," I said. I looked at Jackie. "All along, she knew what Marella was planning. That she was just waiting for a little girl of her own age, trying to get her to come down here, to uncover the bones"—I turned back to Adah—"so that she could live again."

Adah looked at me through large sorrowful eyes.

"You were trying to protect us," I said. I held my hands out to show how helpless we were. "Is it too late to help us? What should we do now?"

"Ted." Jackie tugged at my sleeve to keep me from moving in closer.

Adah indicated herself, then me.

"You're willing to help?" I said, trying to wave Jackie back.

Adah nodded. Once again she gestured toward herself, then toward me.

I pulled away from Jackie and crouched close to Adah. "What?" I said. "What are you saying?"

"Ted," Jackie said more insistently.

Adah simply repeated the same gesture, but then while she had one hand out toward me, she put her other hand on the bones.

I jerked back, knowing that it was too late, that if she wanted to touch me, I was close enough.

She didn't.

"*Te-ed.*" Jackie put two syllables to my name. "Just because Marella is the one who has taken over Vicki, that doesn't mean that Adah doesn't have exactly the same plan for you."

Jackie was right. There was no reason to trust Adah. In fact, it was ridiculous to trust her. If I moved fast enough, there was still a chance I could get away before she could touch me.

I thought of annoying, slobbish Vicki.

I thought of dying and that maybe there wouldn't even be enough of me left to know I was dying.

I thought of the night Vicki had seen what she was sure was a "bad lady" come into my room and how, despite her fear, Vicki had followed her in to warn me.

"But if I don't trust her," I said, speaking to Jackie but looking at Adah, "then there's no way to get Vicki back."

Adah looked down, which I took to mean she agreed but didn't want to say so. She extended her hand to me again and patted the bones with her other hand.

"Ted," Jackie said, "this is crazy."

I took a deep breath. "I hope not," I said.

Much as I didn't want to, I reached down and, with one hand, touched the bones and, with the other hand, touched Adah.

CHAPTER 17

Adah

THE BOY AND I ARE touching the bones at the same time. I feel like something just sucks me up, like a worm feels when the old jaybird sucks it up—*whoosh*, right past the beak, down the throat, and straight into the stomach. I'm dizzy all over, and I'm afraid I'm like to pass out. I put my hand out to keep from tipping right over, and when I catch a sight of that hand, I'm even more like to pass out—the hand is small and white, with no calluses from chopping wood and no burn marks on the back where I always seem to catch my hand on the stove every winter, no matter how careful I plan to be.

I can feel the boy struggling inside me, afraid because he thinks he's given his body over to a haunt and that he'll never get out again.

Easy, honey, easy, I tell him, never having to say the words out loud but just mind to mind because we're in the same body. If I could have talked to Marella this way all these years, everything would have been a lot easier. Or even if I could have talked to the boy this way before, when we were all up at the house, before Marella took things too far.

I open up my mind to him, let him see I mean him no harm. Presently the boy calms down, like when you catch a butterfly in the field and, at first, you can feel it struggling, fluttering against your cupped hands, but then it sits itself down and waits to see what will happen next. The boy sits himself down and waits to see what will happen next.

I look up and there's the girl cousin, the one who looks like a haunt herself. Jaclyn, or Jackie, or Jac, I know she's called, because the boy opens up his mind to me— just for a quick peek, still not sure he trusts me. Jaclyn has picked up two pieces of twigs and holds them out between us, forming a cross, and looks like to faint dead away.

"Calm down, girl," I tell her, touching the cross gently, though my coming so near causes her to shake. "I believe in the Lord Jesus, too."

I start up the hill—marveling, the moment I think on it, that I remember how to walk, how to climb. But the boy's body takes over for both of us. It feels so good to be doing something real. I'd thought I'd never again feel the warmth of the old sun on my face, nor the springiness of the branches on the bushes, a sure sign that warm weather is on the way even though everything looks like winter. Why the good Lord ever made a place as dismal as up North I'll never know. But the air smells crisp. I'd forgotten how good air can smell.

I can hear the girl climbing up the hill behind me, breathing hard like she isn't used to hard work, though she's surely old enough to have babies of her own. When we get to the top, their dog commences to barking. "Quiet down," I tell the hound. "I mean no harm."

The dog just barks and barks and follows as we go into the house.

It isn't as fine as the big house, but there are things of wonder in here, besides the machine that tells stories. There's a chandelier made of metal instead of crystal, but with candles that light themselves, and there are tiny little portraits of the family, painted so real they remind me of the photographs Master had made of himself, 'cept they're in color, and you can't even see the brush strokes. The boy tries to explain, but I tell him, *Hush, now. You don't want me falling in love with your world.* I feel his flutter of fear at *that* thought.

Meanwhile the other boy, the one named Zach or Zachary, calls down from upstairs, "Cinnamon! Quiet! Jackie, what's the matter with that spaz dog of yours?"

I can see him standing in the upstairs hallway, bracing himself, holding on for dear life to a doorknob, 'cept it's metal 'stead of glass, and shiny—shinier even than the Master's brass plate for calling cards. From the other side of that door I can hear a commotion, which is Marella in her new body, causing a fuss, trying to force the door open.

It's so good feeling the springiness of the carpet beneath my feet, running my hand over the smoothness of the wooden banister, seeing all them bright colors. But I say, "Zachary, open that there door for Marella."

His mouth drops open and he looks from me to his cousin, back to me again, and never says a word.

Jaclyn says, "It's all right, Zach." Then she says, "I think."

Still he never says a word but only, presently, lets go of the door.

Marella yanks it right open. "How dare you lock me in there?" she demands, stamping her foot. It isn't her voice, it isn't her face, but, oh, my heart aches to see her and to know that after all this time I can hold her close to me, 'cept that it surely isn't me, either. She has changed from the shirt and trousers the little girl Victoria was wearing into a yellow dress that doesn't even cover her knees. It has embroidered pictures that the boy thinks look like rabbits and baby chicks. From the boy, I recollect what I never knew—that this is Victoria's new Easter dress, which the children's mama bought for her and Victoria complained was too frilly and fussy. But, of course, Marella has never worn anything so fine.

"Marella," I say.

She knows it's me right off. She slams the door shut. The same sort of nonsense she was pulling in the attic, trying to prevent the boy from learning about us and how we got here.

'Cept that Zachary has put his foot in the way, and the door just bounces right back open again.

"Marella," I say, going the rest of the way up them stairs.

"Go away," she calls, backing away from me.

But I grab ahold of her arm. "Marella, you stop this foolishness," I tell her.

"This is my body now," she says, stamping her foot again. Marella was always a child to get that old foot stamping whenever she didn't get her way. "I've waited so long, and now it's mine."

"It is *not* yours," I tell her. "You need to give it back."

"It's mine now," she insists.

"You come over here to me awhile," I say.

But Marella digs the heels of her fine new shoes into the carpeted floor, and the boy's body is not strong enough to force her to move without the risk of hurting her.

But *Zachary* is strong enough. He picks Marella up and tucks her right up under his arm despite all her kicking and fussing, and he says, "Are you sure about this, Jackie?" And she doesn't say anything, so after a while he says to me, "Where do you want her?"

I lead them back down them stairs—Marella and Zachary and Jaclyn and Cinnamon the dog—and into the parlor, what the boy calls the family room.

"You look here," I say to Marella, holding up one of the mirrors that are scattered across the floor.

Marella turns her face away, into Zachary's side, but I take her by the hair at the back of her head and gently but firmly force her to look.

"This is not you," I say. "This is another little girl, by the name of Victoria."

Marella commences to cry, and Zachary places her sitting down on the floor.

I sit down beside her and put my arms right around her, just like I've been hurting to do ever since I first felt this body. I set that old mirror down on the floor, faceup, to remind Marella of who she is.

But she never even looks into it a second time. "It's not fair," she says.

"I know it's not, honey. But this isn't fair, either. Can't you feel how scared that little girl is inside you? She's got her own life to live."

"Just for a little while," Marella says. "You could use their mama's body. It could be just like before, except better."

"No, honey," I say. The boy can tell how much I'm tempted, and I tell him not to fret. I tell Marella, "You've got to come out of there now. We've got a new place to go."

"Not even for a little while?" Marella pleads.

"No," I say. "That would make it even harder to let go. And I'm going to let go," I tell her. "We've stayed too long already. I'm going to let go, and if you don't, you're going to be left behind here, alone, without me. It's only me loving you so hard that's held me back this long."

"I thought you were angry at me," she says. "For standing so near the bank after you told me not to."

"Hush now," I say. "Of all the things I ever felt, I was never angry at you. That's what I stayed to tell you: that I love you." I loosen my hold on the boy. I let myself slip away. I feel like the mist over Tater-field Creek, dissolving in the morning sun.

"Don't go, Mama," Marella whispers, crawling into my lap. "Don't leave me."

I feel her arms tighten around the body which is now more boy than me. I can almost see the new place, and it looks fine.

"I love you, too," Marella says. "I want you to know in case we can't talk where we're going."

But I think we will be able to.

And then I feel her let go of Victoria and come with me.

CHAPTER 18

How Everything Ends

VICKI WAS IN MY LAP, crying. I didn't need to have Adah's impressions to know I had my own sister back again.

Zach and Jackie were watching us warily. "Is it really you?" Zach asked, which wasn't the world's brightest question.

But I figured it meant he'd been worried about me, so I only said, "Yeah. Vicki, too."

We worried and worried over what to do about the bones. It wasn't that we were afraid of Adah and Marella coming back, since the unburied bones had never had anything to do with anything. Still, it just didn't seem right to leave their bones out there in the open. I asked Zach if he thought he could dig a grave, but Jackie pointed out that graves have to be six feet deep or the bones are likely to resurface. Zach said he didn't think he was up to a six-foot-deep hole.

So I called the police. Since the only police officer

I've ever met was the one who came to our school as part of the D.A.R.E. antidrug program, I asked to talk to her.

Naturally Dad came home just as the police were pulling up in front of the house with their lights flashing and their two-way radios crackling. (He was home early because he'd gone out to repair some woman's phone and a dog had bitten him as he'd gotten out of his truck. The woman said she thought he should fix her phone before going to get a tetanus shot because it wasn't her dog. So Dad didn't plan to go back until the next day, even though it was only a small bite.)

Once everybody determined that everybody else was OK, the police told us we couldn't go down into the ditch while they were examining the bones. Like they'd already forgotten who it was that had *found* the bones in the first place. They made us wait in the house, except that Dad didn't. He stood on the edge of the ditch and shouted down questions and advice, which I guess they pretty much ignored.

Eventually—just in time for Mom to come home and get all frantic and be certain that one of her children had fallen down the ditch and died—they brought the bones up. The medical examiner said they were definitely human, obviously old, and that they would be sent to the museum or the university for further testing before burial.

Dad volunteered the information about Great-Great-Grandmother Winifred's journal that I had foolishly shown him, and the next thing I knew they were taking that, too. We're supposed to get it back. Eventually.

Jackie, who'd flipped through to the end, said the last entry was from January 1852, and she insists that in all that time between July and January the only thing Winifred said about helping more runaways was that she'd never do it again.

At first I was real embarrassed for our family because of that, and also on account of Great-Great-Grandfather Theodore not decking that slave catcher for using the word *nigger,* and how, in fact, Theodore used the same word himself. If the police hadn't taken the journal away when they did, I probably would have inked over that section so nobody else would see it.

But now I'm glad I didn't.

It'd be rewriting the past, like those who want to take the word *nigger* out of *Huckleberry Finn* just because the world would have been a nicer place if people had never used that word. Now that I'm keeping this journal of my own, it seems to me that it is only by remembering the past that we can see where we are and how hard a road it has been to get here. If some great-great-grandkid comes along and tries to change my journal around, *I'll* haunt *him.*

Still, I don't think it's rewriting the past to believe that Winifred helped more slaves escape, no matter what she said, because the night she tried to help Adah and Marella there was no secret room to leave her journal in. It must have been built afterward.

What else? Oh, yeah. The Social Studies Fair I missed from being home sick.

My Luxembourg display was set up between Italy and Norway. Tony Malovics had a working model of Vesuvius, and Katie Vanchieri had made a salt-dough relief map of Norway. Luxembourg must have looked pathetic compared to them. I'm told Norway, especially, was very impressive. Katie even added several inches of food-color-blue water to show off the fjords.

At which point, of course, the salt-dough began to dissolve.

Katie didn't notice until the judges were approaching our table, and then, when it was already too late, she picked up the map to get it out of there before it damaged anything.

Which was when Bruce Gelly and Gretchen Prior started tossing Swedish meatballs around.

The next thing anybody knew, Norway had flipped over onto Luxembourg, which fell over onto Italy, causing Vesuvius to erupt prematurely. The table collapsed under the weight of those lunging to protect the displays, and by the time the whole thing was over, Norway, Luxembourg, Italy, and two of the judges were covered with so much lava-colored foam that all three displays were tossed out without even being judged.

I wish I'd been there.

We all got Bs, which Katie is still complaining isn't fair. She says that whatever mark I got, she should have gotten one grade better. Tony's already planning to do another volcano for next year's science fair. And Bruce and Gretchen got so many detentions, they'll probably have to come back after graduation.

In the meantime, I've been working on my mother, telling her how ugly and old the kitchen floor is and that we should rip it up and put in a new one. (I'd hate to have to wait until I inherit the house to see that room.)

AND BY THE WAY, Zach, in case you're snooping through my things again, I finally looked up the word *moor*. It means "a grassy wasteland."

I always knew your definition was stupid.